Baiting the Maid of Honor

A Wedding Dare novel

Tessa Bailey

This book is a work of fiction. Names, characters, places, and incidents are the product of the author's imagination or are used fictitiously. Any resemblance to actual events, locales, or persons, living or dead, is coincidental.

Copyright © 2014 by Tessa Bailey. All rights reserved, including the right to reproduce, distribute, or transmit in any form or by any means. For information regarding subsidiary rights, please contact the Publisher.

Entangled Publishing, LLC
2614 South Timberline Road
Suite 109
Fort Collins, CO 80525
Visit our website at www.entangledpublishing.com.

Brazen is an imprint of Entangled Publishing, LLC. For more information on our titles, visit www.brazenbooks.com.

Edited by Heather Howland and Ellie Brennan
Cover design by Heather Howland

Manufactured in the United States of America

First Edition June 2014

Chapter One

A relaxing, six-day mountain retreat at the exclusive Beaver Creek Resort in Colorado, followed by her best friend's wedding—what could possibly go wrong?

Julie Piper tipped her champagne glass to her lips and smiled at the women conversing animatedly around her. She'd selected the resort's tasteful Osprey Lounge as the venue for Kady's bachelorette party and if her friends' rapidly increasing inebriation served as any sign, it had been a darn good choice. Predinner drinks, a light meal, and a loose seating arrangement had been meticulously planned to make the evening a success. Now she could sit back and enjoy the delicious buzz working its way through her system. It had been far too long since she allowed herself to relax, but there was something soothing about being with three best friends who'd borne witness to four years' worth of triumphs and tragedies in her life. Also known as college.

Kady, the first of them to get hitched, had called with the

news of her engagement a year prior, tearfully asking Julie to be the maid of honor. She'd agreed without hesitation. Among the eclectic mix of four friends, Julie had garnered a reputation as the planner. The maker of pretty things. Energizer Barbie. Not exactly a flattering nickname, but apt nonetheless. She smiled, she mediated, and she decorated. Making people happy was her top priority.

If her smile felt like it might shatter on occasion, well then she supposed even the ceiling in Barbie's Dream House sprang a leak now and again.

Through an avalanche of email and hysterical phone calls between Kady in Colorado and herself in Atlanta, the wedding had been planned down to the tiniest of details. Ask her anything about floral arrangements or canapés and she could dish for days. As she watched Kady show off her ring to the tray-carrying waitress, smile beaming from ear to ear, Julie was reminded why she adored planning and preparation. The end result never disappointed.

Regan, her sorority sister and current New York City headhunter, leaned across the table toward Kady, artfully highlighted hair falling in a wave beside her face. "So does Colton know he's marrying the legendary Tri Delt who once rode a mechanical bull in a bikini and chaps, or did you neglect to mention it?"

"Oh, I told him." Kady sniffed proudly. "He asked to see pictures."

Regan saluted with her glass. "Now there's a man worth giving up casual sex with strangers."

"I seem to remember you taking a turn on that bull, Julie," Kady pointed out.

"I may or may not have pictures of that night," Christine

said on Julie's left, saving her from having to respond. "And I may or may not have brought them along with me to torture you."

Kady's mouth dropped open. "I should have known, Miss Investigative Journalist. Even in those days you were never without your camera."

Christine brushed her bright-red hair over her shoulder, looking quietly pleased. "Always prepared."

"I shudder to think what photographic blackmail you have on me." Regan winced. "I seem to recall some flashes going off the night I scaled the Chi Omega sorority house to steal their mascot off the roof."

Julie nodded sagely. "Mmm-hmm. And nothing between you and the Lord but a smile."

"That's right. I *was* butt-ass naked." Regan flounced back in her chair and shrugged. "Hey, I didn't hear any complaints from below."

As they all groaned over Regan's statement, a new arrival in the lounge caught Julie's eye. Looking horribly out of place, a young woman clutched her purse strap, eyes scanning the room. A vague familiarity about her tipped Julie off. "Kady, is that Colton's sister?"

Kady craned her neck to look toward the bar. "Ooh, yes. Julie, can you go get her?"

Julie had already left the table and was halfway across the room before Kady finished making her request. She flashed her most welcoming smile at a wide-eyed Sophie and pulled her into a hug, laughing when the other girl automatically stiffened like a board. Taking pity on her, Julie moved back a step. "Now, don't let the hugging scare you off, Sophie Brooks. That's just how we do things in the South.

Come on over and let's get you a drink. Are you hungry? They have the most delicious crab cakes. I just about died when I bit into mine."

Sophie's gaze was fastened on Julie's mouth as if she couldn't believe a person could say so many words without taking a single breath. Julie sighed. She was used to that look. "Uh, thank you. No, I'm not hungry." She cracked a nervous little smile. "But I'm more than willing to partake in the drinking."

Julie took her arm and led her toward the table. "Excellent. You're going to fit right in."

The young woman looked doubtful as they approached the table, but as soon as introductions were made and Julie placed a glass of champagne in her hand, the boisterous conversation swelled once more and Sophie seemed to relax slightly, even if she looked like a spectator at a tennis match trying to follow their banter.

Julie waited until everyone had become distracted by bawdy talk of wedding night lingerie choices before she inconspicuously left the table. She floated past the restrooms and the bustling kitchen, and slipped out onto the deserted back patio she'd spied earlier, inhaling the clean mountain air. After nearly missing her flight this morning thanks to a last-minute meeting at her father's company, she'd hit the ground running to get the party set up in time. A breather was definitely in order. As soon as the patio door closed behind her, she yanked the clip out of her hair, letting her long blond hair tumble down around her shoulders. Alone in the darkness, she allowed her ramrod posture to deflate, the tension to ease from her shoulders.

She inched her fingers along her scalp, massaging away

the stress she'd built up over this morning's meeting. Over constant worries she would forget one vital detail and disappoint everyone. Over making tonight special. It felt so good, her eyes closed automatically, head tipping back as a tiny moan escaping past her lips.

"You call that a moan?"

Chapter Two

From his position in the shadows, Reed Lawson watched the blonde spin around on a gasp. When he finally got a good look at her face, it took every ounce of his willpower to retain his casual lean against the stone building. *Fucking gorgeous.* She'd walked out of the restaurant onto the deserted patio, moaning and massaging herself in a way that would put a porn star to shame. Dressed in pink silk that revealed her sun-kissed legs to perfection, he'd been more than happy to let her put on a private show just for him. Until that dress slipped a little too high on those sexy thighs and he'd felt an annoying stab of guilt. Now he wished he'd just gone inside the damn restaurant to the party he was dreading. Wished he hadn't made her turn around.

Because now he wasn't going anywhere. Not until he got an up-close look.

"I'm sorry," she breathed with a Southern twang that oozed old money. "I thought I was out here all alone."

"Don't apologize. I enjoyed the show." He pushed off the wall and stepped into the light, watching as she took his measure. Her chin had gone up a notch at his less-than-gentlemanly comment, making her perusal of him appear condescending, which it likely was. Reed almost laughed. That look had been directed at him so many times, it felt like an old friend. *Yeah, I look more like a criminal than a SWAT team commander. Look your fill, hot legs.* "Maybe I should have kept my mouth shut and seen what happened next."

She gave him a sexy little pout that wasn't designed to make him hard, but it sure as hell had. "You would have been sorely disappointed." The night breeze sent the material of her thin dress swaying over her curves and he almost groaned out loud. Her gaze swept him, head to toe, just as those nipples grew stiff beneath the silk. Did she like what she saw, instead of the usual response he received from girls like her, hightailing it in the opposite direction? Against his will, his interest grew. He was transfixed by her mouth as she spoke again.

"I came out to get some air, not put on a show for some shadow lurker."

One corner of his lips jumped. "Shadow lurker?"

With a sound of irritation, the blonde whirled on her high heels and clicked toward the wooden railing. Disregarding him. Or at least she was making an attempt to do so. Her hands made their way up to that wealth of bright hair again, piling it on top of her head with jerky movements, the delicate muscles of her exposed back shifting in the moonlight. Even from this distance, Reed could see she was tense. About what? *Who cares? Go inside. Leave her be.*

Instead, he found himself wondering what had sent her

out here in the first place. Weren't women who looked like her supposed to *enjoy* parties? Being catered to and flirted with? Served? That final thought brought to mind a vision of her serving him instead, that pouty mouth making magic between his thighs while he instructed her on what he liked.

Jesus. He didn't get the attraction. In her expensive-looking dress and diamond earrings, she practically screamed "pampered and privileged." He'd never gone for that type. Usually went for the exact opposite, actually. Low-maintenance women who knew the score. He didn't have any interest in catering to the whims of some Southern debutante afraid to break a nail in bed. Women like her didn't dirty their hands with men like him. He'd learned that at a very young age growing up on the wrong side of Manchester, Tennessee. It had never bothered him before. He never spared those women a second glance. Now?

He couldn't look away from this one.

She'd wedged a clip between her teeth, attempting to pin her hair up. After several failed attempts, she gave up and let her hands fall to rest on the rail. Reed found himself moving toward her, deciding that once he saw her up close, he'd finally head inside. She wouldn't affect him as much once she hit him with the full force of her snootiness. Those pretty features would transform with distaste and he'd be free to walk.

"Need some help?" The gruff question escaped him before he could stop it, but he was rewarded for asking when she shivered, goose bumps becoming visible along her neck and shoulders. He had to curl his hands into fists to keep from touching her skin. It would be soft. He didn't need a hands-on experiment to determine that, but he goddamn wanted one. *Turn around and roll your eyes at me. Let's get this over with.*

"Help with what?" The sound of wind whispering through the trees nearly swallowed her husky question. "My hair?"

Damn. It hadn't been his imagination. If she hadn't turned tail and traipsed her way back inside by now, this instant attraction didn't end with him. Was it possible a hot-to-trot sex kitten existed under that silk-and-pearls ensemble? Only one way to find out. Settling his hands on either side of her, he brought his body within inches of hers. "I don't do hair, pixie," he rasped against her ear. "Unless you'd like it pulled."

Her indrawn breath sent lust curling in his gut. His cock strained against the front of his dress pants and he wanted more than anything to press her into the railing with his hips. Maybe even pick her up with an arm around her waist and give her a hot little dry run through their clothes. Entice her into the real thing.

Ever so slightly, possibly out of curiosity, she let her back connect with his chest. With difficulty, he managed to stand perfectly still, watching over her shoulder as her breasts rose and fell, that supple flesh swelling over the top of her dress. When she spoke, her voice stoked the fire inside of him, blistering his insides. "Now, why would I want that?"

"If you have to ask, you need it worse than you think."

Hoping like hell the move wouldn't send her screaming, kind of wishing it would, Reed let his fingertips make contact with the top of her back. Still, she didn't turn around or say a damn word to stop him. He couldn't believe it. Not her acceptance of his touch, not the incredible softness he encountered. Who felt like this? Heat rushing through his veins, he very slowly trailed his fingers up her neck and let them tangle in her hair. As he'd seen her do earlier, he massaged her scalp, growling low in his throat when she loosened her neck and let his hand support her head fully. Giving him control. This time, she didn't moan. She panted.

"You'd best stop me now, unless you want to find out what you need."

"I—" He tugged gently so he could see her upturned face and it nearly sent him over the fucking edge. Pink-stained cheeks, damp mouth, heavy eyelids. She looked on the verge of climax, just from his hand in her hair. Christ, who *was* this girl? "I..." she started again, breathlessly.

Reed gripped the strands of her hair and pulled.

A broken sob fell from her mouth as she spun away from Reed, giving him no choice but to let go of her hair. Moonlight spilled over her aroused body, illuminated her shocked face. His instincts told him to reach for her, but common sense kept him rooted to the ground. Finally, *finally*, distaste crept into her expression. For him. Too bad it had come too late. He felt on the verge of imploding with the severe need she'd stirred up in him.

"Are you always this inappropriate?" She spat the words at him. "Even when a lady has shown exactly zero interest?"

"Baby, if that was zero, I can't wait to see what ten looks like."

She laughed a little hysterically. "I guess they'll let just about anyone stay at this resort. Good thing it's big enough I won't have to see you again."

"Good thing," he called after her.

Oh, they would be seeing each other again. Real soon.

• • •

Still buzzing with restlessness and adrenaline after her encounter with the strange man on the patio, Julie rejoined her friends at their table. What in blue blazes had just taken place? Surely she'd dreamed that entire encounter, because ladies didn't let strange men pull their hair. They didn't let *any* man pull their hair, for that matter. And they sure as heck didn't *like* it.

The moment she'd seen him leaning against the building in the darkness should have been the same moment she returned to the party without a backward glance. Instead, the challenge in his eyes had kept her outside. With his hard, commanding form and irreverent air, he'd *wanted* to make her nervous. Expected it. So she'd simply refused. Big mistake. She could still feel his powerful hand in her hair, supporting her, soothing her…then treating her to a combination of unexpected pleasure and pain. The memory of it made her body heat with renewed desire, made awareness spread everywhere it shouldn't. Not for that man whose taunts still rang in her ears.

A series of feminine sighs broke out around the table, drawing her attention. Kady's fiancé, Colton, stood at the entrance flanked by four men as he consulted with the hostess. The groomsmen were crashing the bachelorette party? Her fingers itched to pull out the wedding agenda and remind them they were supposed to be elsewhere, doing man stuff, but Kady's pleased smile stopped her.

"Oh, look! There's my hot chunk of man love now." Kady grimaced. "Sorry, Sophie."

Sophie waved off the apology. "This champagne is definitely softening the blow of hearing you objectify my brother."

"Aw, you're a good sport," Kady said, edging around the table and taking off toward her future husband with open arms, slightly unsteady in her high heels. "Come to mama!"

Her friend's obvious joy easing her unsettled mood, Julie reached for the bottle of champagne, but her hand froze before she could make contact.

No, it couldn't be. The tall, broody shadow lurker from the patio had just joined the group of groomsmen. *He* was the last-minute addition to the wedding party? Quickly, she called to mind the frantic research she'd done on Colton's childhood friend. Reed Lawson, thirty-one. Also known as the gigantic pain in her backside who'd sent her scrambling when he'd agreed to attend the festivities in the eleventh hour. An Atlanta-based SWAT team commander.

Atlanta. The same city she lived in. What were the odds of a chance encounter in the darkness so far from their mutual hometown?

As Colton, the groom, pulled him into a manly, back-slapping embrace, Reed looked over at her and winked.

Chapter Three

With Kady out of earshot, Regan leaned forward in her seat. "All right, tell me about these groomsmen so I can decide on the lucky one who gets to see me naked."

Julie was still recovering from her shock over Reed Lawson and the shadow lurker being one and the same, yet somehow her immediate, anxious internal answer to Regan's question was *not him*. For the second time in one evening, she frowned. That reaction simply wouldn't do. Somehow, after exchanging only a handful of words, he'd found a way to get under her skin, and she wanted him gone. Julie didn't date too often—she simply didn't have the time between work and being a veritable errand girl for her parents—but on the rare occasion she enjoyed the company of a man, manners were minded. Compliments were paid. Frowns never entered the equation.

At once, she could feel a familiar warm tingle at the back of her neck. The same tingle she'd felt on the patio when he approached her from behind. Was he watching her again? It bothered her that she should have such mindfulness for someone she didn't like. She needed to do something about it before it went any further.

"I'm in." She blurted the words, ignoring Christine's surprised and slightly panicked look. "We're on vacation, right? I want to be seen naked, too."

Regan rubbed her hands together. "Things just got interesting."

Julie carefully set her champagne flute down on the glass tabletop. Attempting a casual pose, she draped her arm over the back of her chair and turned slightly to view the men.

Her eyes locked with *his*. And held.

"Looks like Julie's made her pick." Regan laughed while topping off her drink. "You sure about that one? He is tall, troubled, and dangerously sexy. Not your usual type." She tilted her head. "Although maybe he's *exactly* what you need."

Christine cleared her throat, casting a quick glance over her shoulder. "I agree. He's definitely the one you should pick, Julie. So that's settled, right? I vote for a topic change."

Regan and Julie exchanged concerned glances over Christine's odd behavior. It wasn't like level-headed, career-focused Christine to become flustered. "No. It's not settled." Julie quickly scanned the group of men, her gaze landing on a smiling black-haired gentleman with a strapping, athletic build. Based on her painstaking research into the bridal party prior to the wedding, she pegged him as Colton's best man, Logan. He possessed an easy charm, unlike the unapproachable vibe brooding Reed gave off. *Stop thinking about him.* "That one. Logan. Best man, so he's obviously trustworthy. I'll take him." To her right, Sophie choked on her sip of champagne. Julie reached over and patted her on the back. "All right, darlin'?"

"Never better."

Julie started to press, but Regan diverted her attention with an observation of Logan. "Driven, successful, total package. I can see why you'd want to go there. Wish I'd called dibs first, actually."

"You guys aren't really picking out conquests, right?" Christine asked, her cheeks flushed. "Can't we just have a fun, relaxing girls' weekend?"

"If you had the equipment, I'd consider it." Regan sipped her drink, eyes narrowing on the remaining choices. "All right, I'm staying away from Mister Danger. Julie's got her sights set on the best man." She hummed in her throat. "That leaves me with Kady's big bro. I've always found him to be the sweet, strong, silent type."

"I don't think he's sweet at all," Christine snapped, then flushed.

"In that case, I'm *definitely* going with Tyler," Regan said. "I think he's got a certain *je ne sais quoi*. Sophie? You getting in on this?"

Sophie shook her head furiously, short brown bob brushing her chin. "As much as I love a good dare, count me out. The last thing my brother needs at his wedding is his little sister bagging the best man…or, I mean, any of his other best friends. Logan is only one option…"

Julie and Regan exchanged a glance. *Alrighty then.* Julie tipped her chin toward the remaining tan, broad-shouldered man currently laughing loud enough to draw the attention of the entire restaurant. She did a quick mental tally of the groomsmen. "Brock McNeill. Vice president of his family business. Based in Nashville."

Sophie smiled, seeming to relax into her seat. "I haven't seen Brock in years. Along with Reed, aka *Mister Danger*, he grew up in Manchester, where Colton and I spent our summers in Tennessee. The three of them have been friends since I can remember."

Reed. The name really did fit him perfectly. Why that bothered her so much, she couldn't fathom. When she'd begun gathering information on the bridal party, he'd been the sole question mark; his name hadn't even been provided on Kady and Colton's guest list. *Possible groomsman*. She hadn't bothered checking into him. Who decides to join a bridal party at the last minute? "So you must know an awful lot about them. What are they like?" She fluttered her hands. "Just a little something to help Regan choose between Tyler and Brock." *Not because I want to know more about Reed.*

Sophie crossed her arms over her middle and spoke hesitantly. "One summer I caught them out by the lake reading a *Hustler* magazine. Brock likes women with breasts the size of flotation devices. Reed...harder to tell with him, but he tended toward brunettes."

Julie set down her glass a little harder than intended. "*Fine*."

"Fine, what?" Regan asked.

"Fine...make your choice. Bachelor one or two?"

Avoiding Reed's steady gaze, Julie took a good look at Brock, already knowing Tyler well enough from her years of friendship with Kady. She tipped her chin toward Brock. "That there, Regan, is a Southern boy. I don't even need to hear him say two words. And as my Aunt Sylvie would say,

Southern boys are slicker than pig snot on a radiator."

Sophie grimaced. "My God. How would pig snot get on a radiator in the first place?"

"I don't know, but the expression had to originate somewhere."

Regan nodded. "I think you're right about Brock. He's got 'arrogant playboy' written all...oh my God. He's staring at my boobs!"

Julie saluted with her glass. "Southern boys."

Christine abruptly pushed her chair back, looking paler than before. "I-I need some air. I can't *breathe* in here."

Regan tried to st Christine with a hand on her arm. "How much did you drink?"

"Apparently not enough," Christine responded. She and Regan had a hushed, heated conversation before Regan let her go. Christine made a beeline for the exit.

Concerned over her friend's abrupt departure, Julie stood to go after, but was stayed by Kady's sudden reappearance. "Girls, come on over and meet the groomsmen. Hands off the groom himself, but otherwise it's open season."

Chapter Four

Reed watched his little blond pixie shake hands with Logan, the best man he'd met a little over an hour ago. He'd seemed a decent sort, but Reed suddenly couldn't stand the sight of him. Not with the way *she* looked up at him, a flirtatious smile playing at the edges of her lips. *She*, being the one who'd been putting him through an excruciating round of torture ever since she let him pull her hair out on the patio, forcing a sexy-as-hell sob from her delicious-looking mouth. Now her smooth, mile-long legs were on display for every male in the vicinity to ogle and fantasize about. It wasn't working for him.

He'd been dreading the idea of this loud party. Making small talk with people he'd likely never see again once this week ended. He'd even considered heading back to his room and waiting for a less formal event to make his entrance. The *last* thing he'd expected was a blond bombshell to moan her way into his head, making him hard as a rock in the process.

She'd run away from him too soon, disappearing before he could ask her…what exactly? If she'd be willing to hike that dress a little higher and let him see how long those legs went on for? He'd love to ask her that question. Just to see if she'd give him that same sexy pout she'd intended as a set-down outside. The one that turned him on like hell instead.

Matter of fact, her dress *did* seem shorter than it had on the patio. Was it his imagination or had she hiked it up to drive him insane?

If she gave him the slightest encouragement, he'd have sucked that pouty lower lip between his teeth so he could swallow her next moan. Explain to her in no uncertain terms the effect her legs were having on him and every man inside the goddamn restaurant, before tugging the dress up over her hips and giving her a physical demonstration.

Such urgent need for one particular woman was completely unlike him. His outward demeanor warned off all but a certain type of woman and she did not, in any way, shape, or form, fit that description. Reed's tastes tended toward women who could take a little manhandling. Begged for it, even. Oftentimes, women sensed his overwhelming need for control, struggling to be let loose inside him, and they approached him first. Being that Reed preferred keeping his conquests impersonal, fast and hard suited him perfectly. So did never looking back.

This being the case, the fact that he'd felt a flare of panic when she'd run from him didn't sit well. He'd actually battled the urge to go after her. His desire to return to his room had ceased to be a possibility. Instead, he'd rounded the building and entered the Osprey Lounge, already anxious to see her again. Those gorgeous legs, elegantly crossed, had drawn his eye immediately and he hadn't looked away once since then.

With her manicured hand resting on Logan's forearm, she tossed back her head and laughed, flawless skin catching the candlelight. His fingers curled into his palm and squeezed. First, when the hell had he started noticing trivial details like candlelight? Second, she might not be his type, but if she didn't stop laughing and flashing those wide blue eyes up at Golden Boy, he was going to carry her out of the lounge draped over his shoulder kicking and screaming.

It had been a long time since he'd felt his control slipping. He'd left that aspect of his personality behind him long ago before joining the force in Atlanta. After shedding his hell-raiser image, his energy had been channeled into work. Nothing riled him. Until her. Hell, he didn't even know her name and had only spent a few minutes with her. What the hell was the matter with him?

"Easy now, big boy," his best friend Brock drawled at his elbow. "There are enough bridesmaids for each and every one of us poor, wretched souls." He tipped back his beer, eyes full of humor. "How would you feel about a midweek swap?"

Reed jerked his chin toward the pixie. "Name."

"Now, how would I know? We haven't been here but five minutes."

He cast a skeptical look at his friend, who rarely entered a room without gathering stats on every available female.

Brock rolled his eyes. "Julie Piper. Maid of honor. Five foot…six? Hard to tell in those heels. Cute little peach of a thing, ain't she?"

Reed grunted. "No swaps."

"Hell, you're no fun." Brock feigned disappointment.

"You planning on letting her sweet-talk Logan all night or you going to make a move?"

Julie's gaze collided with his before flitting away once more. The simple look had the aftereffect of a sucker punch to the jaw. "When I'm ready. She's not going anywhere with him."

"Is that right? I know a woman with a plan when I see one." He tipped his beer bottle in Julie's direction. "That one's got a plan."

Reed's eyes narrowed on Julie and admitted Brock had a point. She'd started shifting on her feet like she stood on hot coals. Her fluttery hand gestures were growing more dramatic by the second. As if on cue, he watched as her hand covered a momentarily distracted Logan's room key where it sat on their shared table, and slid it neatly into her purse. Reed's entire body tensed.

"Told you."

"It's not fucking happening."

Brock checked his watch. "You better work fast. Women with plans wait for no man."

"Says the expert."

"Hate to brag."

Goddammit. How the hell had he ended up at some ritzy resort wearing loafers, lusting after some sorority girl? Just this morning, he'd fallen into bed at 3:00 a.m. after his SWAT team, of which he'd recently been promoted to commander, performed a middle-of-the-night arrest in the College Park section of Atlanta. He'd been filthy, exhausted, and slightly more jaded than when he'd left the house that morning. Just the way he liked it. He was here because his best friend was getting married; otherwise he wouldn't be within ten feet of this many suits.

He owed Colton. That's why he was here. Since he didn't have the ability to articulate how much the other man's friendship had meant to him all those years ago, he would grin and bear the endless parade of hors d'oeuvres and stock market talk.

And come hell or high water, he'd have the girl.

As Reed's mind began formulating and discarding different ways to keep Julie from her obvious plan to sneak into Logan's room later in the evening, apart from threatening Logan with bodily harm that is, his cop's sense began picking up on other dramas playing out in the lounge. Tyler, the bride's brother, had fallen deathly silent upon walking in, eventually grumbling some excuse to leave. Sophie, Colton's little sister, had cast a couple nervous glances toward Logan before slipping out of the restaurant like a ninja. The best man looked too tired to even notice. That made him feel marginally better about him rising to the occasion with Julie, but he wasn't taking any chances.

A flashy brunette entered his line of vision, interrupting his train of thought. She looked almost as out of place as Reed felt, her expensive clothing and citified demeanor belonging far away from the mountains of Colorado. When the newcomer smiled up at him, Reed tossed a quick look over her shoulder and watched Julie tense. Good. She wasn't as indifferent as she let on.

Reed raised an eyebrow at the brunette. "Can I help you?"

"I'm Regan. You don't know me but I'm about to become your favorite person in the world," she said without disrupting her smile. "Give me your room key."

"Come again?"

"It's not for me. Although you should be so lucky." She tossed her hair over her shoulder and held out her hand. "You're just going to have to trust me."

Brock, edging in between them, held his hand out toward Regan. "It's nice to meet you, sweetheart. I'm Brock."

"There's nothing sweet about me," she responded with a mocking smile, then looked back at Reed. "You've got five seconds. Five…four…"

"Women with plans," Brock muttered beside him.

Reed reached into his pocket and drew out the key. Eyes narrowed, he dropped it into Regan's palm and crossed his arms over his chest. He didn't like having orders tossed at him, but he was curious.

"Good choice," she threw over her shoulder as she clicked away on her sky-high heels.

Reed and Brock watched in silence as Regan joined Julie and Logan's conversation. With an arm draped over Julie's shoulders, she appeared to be regaling them with a funny story. Reed couldn't help but smile when her fingers slipped inside Julie's purse and replaced *his* room key with Logan's, just in time for her story to wrap up. Without a backward glance, she sailed off toward the bar.

"That's one hell of a woman," Brock remarked beside him.

"Careful. She's trouble."

"Uh-huh. The good kind."

With a shake of his head, Reed turned his attention back to Julie, trying to decide how he felt about being on the receiving end of a seduction meant for someone else. She held a fresh glass of champagne in her hand and she'd started squinting at Logan as if she couldn't see him quite clearly in her tipsy state. Why he found that trait...insanely cute...he couldn't begin to imagine. What he *didn't* find cute at all was the way she'd begun swaying toward Logan, using his arm for balance.

She'd clearly reached her limit for the night and Reed didn't take advantage of women. But the alternative was someone else taking advantage of her, and he couldn't allow that either. He'd let her come to him in the dark, thinking he was Logan. Then he'd erase Golden Boy from her memory completely.

When Julie said her good-byes and left the lounge, anticipation heated his belly. He tossed back the remaining third of his beer and headed for his room. To wait for his girl.

Chapter Five

Julie's bare feet sank into the carpeted hallway as she crept toward Logan's room. Halfway there, she'd noticed her lack of footwear, but for the life of her couldn't remember taking off her heels. And in her happily buzzed, slightly groggy state, going all the way back seemed like an awful lot of effort. Julie cast a look over her shoulder, looking for—what? Was she hoping someone would stop her? Give her an excuse to turn back?

She prowled down the hallway with renewed determination. A full-grown woman feeling guilty about good old-fashioned sex. Just plain pitiful. That's all it would be. Two consenting adults blowing off a little steam.

Her head dropped forward as she failed to convince herself. If she'd been comfortable with the notion of casual sex, she would have come right out and asked Logan for it in the lounge, instead of skulking around the resort like some kind of cartoon robber. She'd never been good at this sort of thing. After consuming a bottle of champagne, the idea of sneaking in and out of Logan's room, remaining hidden in the dark during the entire physical transaction, had seemed like a genius plan. No small talk or awkward attempts at seduction. She wouldn't have to worry about which way to tilt her head or if she was smiling too much. In the dark, none of that would matter. She'd been so sure of her strategy, but now that the moment grew near, she felt her courage waning.

Well, that was half the reason for her hesitation, anyway.

The other half stood approximately six foot three inches tall and oozed irreverence from every pore. Reed. He hadn't taken his eyes off her once in the lounge, except to address Regan. She'd liked being the center of his attention. Which didn't make a darn lick of sense. Their acquaintance so far had been brief, but she was certain of one thing.

She didn't like him. With the thought came another uneasy glance over her shoulder.

Julie would be the first to admit her life had been easy. She'd grown up privileged and given many advantages. Throughout her life, she'd encountered the look permanently etched on Reed's face. Disdain. Mockery. He probably assumed he kept every thought hidden, but she could read him like a book. This entire wedding and all its frippery was an inconvenience to him and for some reason, he'd decided to make her the source of his annoyance.

Yet here she stood outside Logan's door, thinking about Reed instead. All the more reason to knock on Logan's door and put the giant bastard out of her mind. Involuntarily, she winced at thinking the word "bastard," even if she hadn't said it out loud. Her Aunt Sylvie would skin her alive for having such an unladylike thought. Tomorrow she would try to find Reed's silver lining, Julie resolved with a nod. No sense in holding on to any hostility when she was determined to relax and enjoy the weekend with her rarely seen friends. If she felt any attraction for him, well, that would end tonight. Once she seduced another man in the dark…without any discussion beforehand, Reed would be out of her head. She just needed to go on in and have the sex.

Julie glanced down at the key in her palm, which she'd squeezed so hard, it had left an imprint. *Stop being a coward. You're a good girl every second of your boring life. You wanted to step outside your comfort zone? Here is your opportunity.* With a fortifying breath, she slid the key into the lock. Then she hesitated. Did she want to do this? Obnoxiously, Reed's image swam through her mind once more. It wouldn't be right, would it? To seduce one man while thinking of another? She started to remove the key, but the door swung open.

A big hand snaked out through the opening and pulled her inside. Before she could utter a single word, the door slammed shut and her back hit the hard wood. In a split second, she'd gone from the bright hallway to complete darkness and it took her a moment to get her bearings. The quick movement made the champagne in her system kick up a bigger fuss than two grannies competing in an apple pie bake-off.

As she attempted to steady herself, she felt warm hands circle her bare ankles. At once, awareness raced up her calves and weakened her knees. Her breath hitched in her throat as those hands stroked higher up the backs of her legs, fingers dragging lightly on her skin and shooting lightning to her core. Higher, until they reached her thighs, which were already flexing in anticipation. Then she felt damp pressure trail over the inside of her knee. A mouth? When the unmistakable sensation of a tongue licked over the flesh of her inner thigh, she slumped back onto the door with a breathy moan.

Briefly, she wondered why this felt so right, when seconds ago, the idea of being with Logan had felt infinitely wrong. Rational thought fled as seeking, greedy hands followed the tongue's path, kneading and smoothing as they went. They could have only one destination. She needed to be touched there so badly, she ached beyond the barrier of her panties, where she'd grown increasingly wet. Julie's thighs began to part when it registered how fast they were moving. How, in mere seconds, she'd gone from seducer to *seduced*. Before the door opened, she'd had every intention of backing out, yet now this man's touch had transformed her into a willing participant. His roughness felt unfamiliar, but her body responded as though it had been...*expecting* this kind of treatment from someone.

Just not from Logan.

From Reed, though...yes. Her heartbeat accelerated as the hands, the mouth on her legs became his. *Oh, God.* Lust twisted in her belly. A man like Reed would move fast, give her one choice only. To receive pleasure. She shouldn't like it. Shouldn't need it. And this wasn't Reed touching her, it was Logan. *Logan.* Confusion shone through the growing need. They needed to slow down so she could figure out where it was coming from.

She stayed his ascending hand with her own. "W-wait. Aren't you going to..."

His growl of frustration vibrated against her thigh and she sucked in a breath. Julie's brow furrowed as she heard the noise. A noise so unlike the congenial best man. Was it possible she'd misjudged him? She thought they were two like-minded people, interested in polite, tidy sex, but maybe she'd been mistaken. That's what she got for judging a book by its cover. Once again, an image of Reed popped into her mind, but she determinedly stowed it away.

"Aren't you going to at least kiss me first?" No answer. "I'm not playing coy or anything, mind you…I just reckon, well, that it's the decent, honest thing to do is all. Under the circumstances."

He sighed loudly and she felt him rise to his feet. His larger frame crowded her against the door, fitting them together in a way that was blatantly indecent. She felt his arousal, thick at her belly. Her breasts flattened against his chest in a way that felt sinful and divine simultaneously. Warm breath puffed out against the top of her head.

"Kissed where?" His voice was a rough, almost inaudible whisper that bathed her in blistering heat. "Your mouth? Or the slick little pussy you're hiding from me?"

Julie gasped loudly in the darkness, her entire world tilting on its axis. No one had ever dared to speak to her in such a crude manner. She opened her mouth to demand an apology when a loud sound echoing in the room brought her back to reality. She realized it was her own heavy, panting breath. No. No way. It couldn't have turned her on. She couldn't actually *like* his foul words. Could she? Her body hummed like a swarm of bees, the body she continued to press against him so very intimately. Begging for even more contact.

What are you going to do, Julie? Walk away when you're finally feeling something with a man? When someone has finally succeeded in evoking an emotion other than mild interest?

"Both." She swallowed hard, unable to keep the image of Reed at bay this time. His mouth. His tongue. She wanted them so bad it pained her. "Kiss me in both places."

She felt a ripple of shock go through him, and her body answered it. With a loud groan, his mouth came down on hers, hard and punishing. He kissed her almost angrily, forcing her lips apart and sweeping his tongue inside in a way meant to provoke her. Incite her. Julie couldn't get enough of his hard mouth moving like a brand over hers. She dug her fingers into the collar of his shirt and tugged him down as she pushed higher on her toes to meet him. They kissed furiously until breath ran scarce, pausing to draw air and bite at each other's lips. Not one single coherent thought could be formed around the heat coursing through her, concentrated on the apex between her legs. She felt needy, out of control, *hot*. With a sound of frustration, she clutched his shoulders and hitched her legs up around his waist.

An animalistic sound tore from his throat as his hips notched firmly between her thighs. Julie opened her mouth to issue a demand for more pressure, but her backside slammed into the door with the force of his thrust before she could voice her need. She cried out into the encompassing darkness as he growled into her neck.

"More. More. More."

"More what, baby?" His grated whisper sent electricity racing down her spine. "This?" He hooked his arms beneath her knees and spread her legs so wide Julie winced at the twinge of pain. Then he positioned the bulging length that pressed insistently behind his fly over her sensitive flesh and grinded her back against the door. Teeth sank into her shoulder as he drove himself against her over and over. Julie dimly registered the sounds of the door bumping and squeaking in its frame with each potent, demanding thrust. Pleasure, foreign and intense, spiraled through her system, rendering her incapable of anything but feeling. Taking what he'd correctly judged she needed. Her thighs tightened around his waist as she felt the dam inside of her giving way. She bit her lip and absorbed five more thrusts, his erection sliding with a mind-numbing friction over the sensitive part of her still shielded by silk underwear. Then she lost her grip on the present, sensations imploding within her like a ticking time bomb. She squeezed his hips between her legs and rode out her orgasm, his hands digging into the flesh of her bottom to help her get as close as humanly possible while her hips bucked.

His hard mouth worked over hers, swallowing her strangled cries, growling and thrusting his tongue deep with each of her frantic movements. When she came down from her climax, breath racing in and out past her lips, she heard his muffled whisper at her ear. "Oh baby, I could have come, just like this. With your fuck-me thighs opened up wide for me on the door. Now?" He laughed darkly. "Nothing will satisfy me unless I taste all that heat first."

As he levered her against the door with his body and began to strip off his shirt, a tingle of uncertainty raced over Julie's skin, almost enough to blot out the unmistakable longing. She somehow battled the latter feeling and focused on his words. Since she'd entered the room, he hadn't spoken above a whisper, but nothing he'd said so far had been reminiscent of the man she'd mingled with over cocktails an hour earlier, making polite small talk. Perhaps when a man this sexually intense became aroused, his voice altered slightly? She didn't have the experience to know, but he was making it too easy for her to picture Reed in his place, when she shouldn't be sparing him a thought. But she was. Couldn't stop.

Julie wanted so badly for her theory to be true. That Logan became a different type of man in the dark. She didn't want this to end. But her instincts sent her hands over his shoulders, exploring, testing. Had Logan been this big? Just beneath his shoulder blade, she felt it. A large, jagged scar. Not the kind of mark even a marginally competent surgeon would leave. Logan's bare back had been featured in billboards for his sporting goods company...and he certainly had no scar.

"W-who are you?" No sooner had the words left her mouth than she knew. The hints and red flags she'd patently ignored flashed in front of her eyes like fireworks.

His teeth traced the column of her neck and she struggled to keep from tilting her head to give him better access. He pushed up hard against her damp center. "You know who it is. You've known all along, haven't you, pixie?"

Reed. If the nickname hadn't clued her in, she still would have known his identity beyond a shadow of a doubt as soon as he spoke above a whisper. His baritone voice resonated within her. Julie's heart pounded wildly in her chest as she pondered his question. If she was honest with herself, she hadn't been attracted to the successful best man, gorgeous though he might be. But the second *this* man's hands had touched her legs in the dark, she'd turned into a shivering mass of hormones. Had she been aware of his actual identity? Perhaps not consciously, but deep down she knew she'd purposefully ignored the warning signals her brain had given off. She'd been too lost in the heat to let reality intrude.

Then it hit her. What Reed had done. Allowed her to sneak in and seduce him. *The wrong man.*

Julie shoved him with all her might and nearly collapsed onto the floor when his wall of support left her body. Her hand fumbled along the wall, searching for a light switch. When she found it, she flipped it on and spun to face him. She opened her mouth to scream every obscenity she could muster up, but his intense expression distracted her. Then her gaze dropped from dangerously narrowed hazel eyes to the body beneath…and she forgot to breathe. At least a dozen tattoos stretched over hardened muscle, some of them disappearing beneath the waistband of his low-slung dress pants. Two scars bisected his abdomen and pectoral muscles, adding to his already considerable air of danger. Big hands flexed at his sides, tightening into fists when she merely continued to stare at the most painfully masculine physique she'd ever witnessed outside of the naughty emails Regan often sent her.

"Would you like me to take off my pants now so you can really be impressed?"

His gruff question jolted Julie out of man-candy fantasyland and she dragged her gaze up from the large swell behind his fly, trying desperately to ignore the needy tightening in her belly. It enraged her that she could still feel desire for him after the stunt he'd pulled. "By all means, take the pants off. It'll make it much easier when I castrate you."

Julie ignored the fluttering in her chest when his full lips tilted at the ends, his amusement vanishing just as quickly. "Now that would be one hell of a shame." He took a measured step in her direction. She refused to give up any ground when he stopped a breath away and dragged his teeth over his bottom lip, eyes tracking over her heaving breasts. "You were enjoying it so much a minute ago. When you rode it like you owned it."

"Lord, would you please stop talking to me like that? It's just not right." She dragged a shuddering breath into her lungs and raised a hand to keep him backed off. Any closer and she might be tempted to lick one of those tattoos. And just where had *that* thought come from? Julie Piper didn't lick tattoos. She licked the odd Popsicle on a hot Atlanta day. Maybe a cherry lollipop on Halloween. Not a depiction of a charging bull underneath the words…what was that? Latin? Huffing a frustrated breath, Julie massaged her forehead, trying to focus on anything but the pent-up sexual energy radiating from the man in front of her. It practically spilled from every inch of his skin, heating her where she stood. He needed to be put back in his place. She straightened her spine and looked him in the eye. "You knew I didn't come here to see you. You let me think you were Logan."

Whoa mama. That certainly worked. Reed's demeanor transformed from ready-to-play to outrageously pissed before she could blink. He visibly reined himself in, but she could tell it wasn't easy. She could see the effort maintaining his control cost him. "Listen to me, pixie. You can pretend all you want that you didn't love my eyes on you all damn night when I couldn't stop imagining your beautiful legs draped over my shoulders. You can pretend to be indifferent toward me in front of all your giggling girlfriends." He braced a hand on the wall above her head and leaned in close. "But don't pretend, not for one goddamn second, that you thought it was Golden Boy ringing your bell. You knew exactly who was between your thighs. You've wanted me there for hours. I just found a way to give us what we both wanted." He gave a frustrated shake of his head. "Well, one of us, anyway. I'm still hard enough to cut through steel."

"I didn't...*don't* want you," Julie whispered shakily. Even to her own ears, it sounded like an obvious lie, but she was still reeling crazily from his provocative speech to make a better effort. "You have a wild imagination, though. Honestly, I wouldn't have guessed it." She cleared her throat, trying to make her suddenly hoarse voice return to normal. "I only responded that way because I thought you were someone else."

Reed's jaw flexed. "That so? Put your money where your mouth is, then. All the lights are on now. Let's see how you respond when you know who's making you come."

Julie didn't know what to say. No way could she take him up on such a challenge. Even if her mind insisted on denying the attraction, her body knew if Reed touched her, she'd boil hotter than a teakettle. Might even whistle. Within minutes, he would prove her claim incorrect. Have her shamefully begging and moaning up against the door once again.

She laid her hand on the doorknob. "Such a gracious and eloquent offer, but I'm going to have to pass. I wasn't interested *before* and I'm certainly not interested *now*, especially after this little Houdini After Dark magic act."

When she pulled open the door, his fingers curled around her elbow, bringing her to a stop. She didn't turn around to face him, but she could feel his lips moving in her hair. "I'm going to let you get away with the lie tonight, pixie, since I made you come hard enough that I'll be able to relax. For now. But I need to make one more thing crystal clear before you leave." He traced her ear with his tongue. "If you need servicing while we're stuck in this fancy-ass hotel for a week, I'm going to be the one to do it. No one else. Not Golden Boy. Not even your right hand." He let go of her arm and she swayed, frowning when he laughed under his breath. "And when you slip between your sheets tonight, think about this. I will service you so hard you'll be booking another week here just to recover."

Julie slipped out into the hallway and walked toward her room down the hall without remembering a single step of her journey to get there.

Chapter Six

Reed strode purposefully down the hotel corridor, his mood best described as surly. Although to be fair, the description fit him on his best day. Today, however, his frustration had a name, an ass that didn't quit, and lips he'd spent the better potion of the night envisioning inching down his stomach.

Julie Piper. A hellcat disguised as Tinker Bell.

After the condition she'd left him in last night, he'd woken from his shitty attempt at sleep with the intention of finding her and laying more groundwork. Whatever the reason, he wanted the stuck-up rich girl in his bed. Like *hell*. And when something pulled him from his casual indifference long enough to make him want it, he went after the damn thing with single-minded determination.

It was this driven intensity that had pulled him out of the backwoods slums of rural Tennessee and made him a SWAT team leader in bustling Atlanta. A position he didn't take lightly or for granted. He knew how easily his life could have gone the other way. If he'd let it.

Yes, Reed didn't make a habit of allowing obstacles to come between him and the thing he wanted. However, this appeared to the first time that specific some*thing* was a some*one*. He didn't have time to question the anomaly, though. Not if he wanted enough time to work the blonde out of his system. He had a feeling it would take longer than a week to rid himself of the clawing lust she'd cursed him with, but a week was all he had. Time was of the essence. If avoiding him was her plan, he would simply have to make it difficult for her.

After breakfast, he'd gone for a three-mile run outside on the resort grounds in an attempt to dull the sexual frustration. It hadn't worked. Not at all. He figured unless he could get Julie to give in to their mutual need, he'd wear out the soles in his sneakers before the week ended.

Jesus, the way she'd pumped those hips as she came… Reed gritted his teeth at the memory. He'd wanted to push those panties to the side and give her a good, hard fuck against the door. The first in a series of many good, hard fucks he planned on giving her. The only thing that held him back was the chance that she actually thought he was Logan. Oh, he knew she'd convinced herself of it, at least partly. Call him arrogant, but he knew when a woman was interested in what he had to offer. Julie was interested. Now he had to convince her of that.

The alternative would be to abandon the chase. Let her and Golden Boy hook up, like everyone probably assumed they would. Hell, they looked like a goddamn Banana Republic advertisement standing next to each other. Reed paused in the center of the lobby, deciding which direction he would take to find Julie. He also took that moment to erase the image of Julie and Logan together. He'd never been jealous a day in his life, not over a woman. The feeling had to go and there was only one way to get rid of it.

Realizing he had no clue where Julie would be in the middle of the day, he drew his wedding itinerary out of his jeans pocket with a heavy sigh. He was carrying around a damn *wedding itinerary*. On pink and gold stationery with the words "True love doesn't have a happy ending because it never ends" in raised script along the top. God help him if his team ever saw it. The very idea made him feel ill.

His gaze narrowed on the list. The next planned meeting wasn't until six o'clock. *Wine and Dine Welcome at Spago*. Reed groaned inwardly. He'd rather chug nails. Would it be so much to ask for a Beers and Wings night? Or an Everyone Plan Your Own Shit Because We're All Adults and Don't Require a Glittery Schedule night?

He considered his options. He could go check her room, although he wasn't likely to find her there in the middle of the afternoon. Turning on his heel, he headed in the direction of Spago. Julie didn't seem the type to sit still for five minutes. Her being the maid of honor and all, he had a feeling he would find her already decorating for tonight's event, unable to stop herself from being a way hotter version of Martha Stewart. A walk to the other side of the hotel proved his theory correct. When he ducked under the doorjamb into the lounge, he found her halfway up a ladder hanging a string of garden lights. Her calf muscles flexed as she pushed higher to reach the ceiling, her dress billowing mid-thigh.

His pulse kicked up at the thought of surprising her with

his tongue trailing up her thigh. He could love her with his mouth right where she stood. Reluctantly, he decided against it. If he startled her and she fell off the ladder, it wouldn't exactly help his cause. Having made the decision to wait until she descended, Reed leaned against the doorjamb and watched her impatiently as she changed the placement of the lights six different times. Then her cell phone rang, making her jump and wobble on the ladder. Reed sprang forward, but she caught herself in time and answered on the third ring. He slumped back against the door with a slowly released breath.

"Yes, Mother. Still in Colorado. I'll be here for the week, remember? Kady is getting m—" She paused and he watched her shoulders slump a little. "No, I...I'm sorry. I didn't realize you were counting on me to drive you to the church tonight... Yes, I'm aware Serena always made time to take you." The lights fell to the ground from Julie's suddenly lifeless fingers and Reed frowned. He didn't like the tone her voice had taken on. It bothered him much more than it should. He resisted the urge to pull her down off the ladder and shake her until she smiled. A thought unlike him in every way. He wanted only one thing from her mouth, and it definitely wasn't a smile.

Head tipping back, Julie sighed. "You're right, Mother. Serena was one of a kind. Not everyone can be that perfect. Myself included."

When Julie hung up, she stood stock-still on the ladder for several long moments. Reed couldn't take her deflated posture anymore and cleared his throat into the silence, moving toward her in case she startled. She turned abruptly, blue eyes wide and damp, but didn't fall. All at once, her chin went up and her mouth flattened in warning. He watched her process the fact that he'd overheard the call, not allowing himself to feel the creeping regret when her cheeks flamed and she averted her eyes, looking embarrassed.

Once again, the pit in his stomach widened. He wanted the girl from last night back. The one who'd threatened to cut off his balls. The one who'd kissed him with unleashed enthusiasm, legs wrapped around his hips like a steel vise. And damn it, for some unnamed reason he wanted to help her save face. If anyone knew about parents piling shit on the heads of their children, it was him. There was only one way to take away the hurt: replace it with something else. A hot Southern temper would do nicely.

"I can see your light-pink panties from down here, pixie girl. You waiting for me to reach up and sneak them off?" He made a hungry sound in his throat, circling the ladder without removing his gaze from between her legs. "From this angle, I could learn all your secrets. Come on, let's see that sweet spot you're hiding. Show me where my mouth will go to drive you fucking crazy."

· · ·

Julie's breath felt trapped in her lungs. Every inch of her skin flamed hot, like it had been licked with fire. All remnants of frustration from her mother's phone call seeped from her body as Reed launched his verbal attack from below. His gaze felt like a tangible thing. She felt it brush between her thighs as though he'd used his hand instead of hooded hazel eyes. When she recognized her desire to part her thighs even farther so he could look his fill, she sucked in a breath and descended from the ladder angrily. How dare he listen in on her phone call, then address her as though she hadn't already turned down his advances once and for all? Regardless of the fact that she'd spent a restless night in her massive hotel bed, imagining what would have happened if she'd actually stayed in Reed's room, he had no right being here now, discussing her lady parts like they were the soup of the day.

"Now you listen to me and you listen well, *Mister* Lawson." She got right up in his face and pushed a finger into the center of his chest. When his mouth twitched at one end it only made her angrier. "If your mama didn't see fit to teach you basic manners, that's none of my concern, but that racket isn't welcome around here." She took back her finger and smoothed a hand down her skirt. "I assure you, my sweet spot will remain a secret to you, no matter what rolls off your tongue."

"Is that a fact?"

"Set in stone."

"Come closer, then." He crooked his finger at her. "Let me talk in your ear for a while and we'll see if you can keep your secrets, pixie."

"Stop calling me that. It's ridiculous and unfitting," she huffed, amazed at how much she wanted to take him up on his offer. Oh, God, she wanted to feel the way she had last night. So bad. But it would be a cold day in hell before she gave in to his arrogant demands. Honestly, he acted as if her acquiescence was a foregone conclusion. Women must not turn him down very often. Why the thought only served to rile her temper, Julie didn't care to explore. "I'm not interested. Keep your hands and thoughts to yourself."

She could practically hear his jaw grinding. "How can I help you hang those lights if I keep my hands to myself?"

"I don't recall asking for your help."

"You're getting it anyway."

"When was the last time someone told you *no*, Mr. Lawson?"

"*Reed*." He scooped the lights off the floor and handed her one end. "And I don't recall."

Julie took the end he offered and climbed the ladder once more. When his attention dropped to her legs, she arched her eyebrow and indicated the opposite end of the room where more lights waited to be hung. After a moment when he looked to be debating whether or not to follow her instructions, he went with a sigh.

"How did you get stuck doing this?" he muttered, fishing through a wooden crate.

"Stuck?" She frowned. "I love doing this."

"Jesus. What the hell for?"

Julie opened her mouth to reply, then realized no one had ever asked her that question. She'd always been a planner, an idea girl. But until her sister's death four years ago, the planning had only been for fun events. Now, it applied to everything. Her parents, especially her mother, had taken Serena's death hard and she'd been required to step up. Not only event planning for her father's company, but helping her parents run their estate. Everything Serena had done so well. This kind of planning? This was pure pleasure, even if the strain of making everything perfect got to her from time to time.

After giving it careful thought, she answered slowly. "I suppose I like seeing people enjoy themselves, knowing I had a little something to do with it. Mood, lighting, and ambiance can make or break a party. Kady is a good friend and she deserves the best. That's why."

Reed made a noise in his throat.

"I don't expect you to understand."

"I understand the last part. Maybe." He scowled at a curly pink ribbon that had attached itself to the end of his hammer. "But don't you think we'd have an equally good time tipping back a few cold ones? Throwing a few hot dogs on the grill?"

"Maybe you haven't had a chance to read your wedding itinerary thoroughly yet, but we *do*, in fact, have an outdoor soiree planned—"

"The word 'soiree' has no place near a grill."

Julie pushed a tack into the wall using a little too much force and bent it. "No one is forcing you to go. I'm certainly not going to take attendance." She turned with a hand perched on her hip. "If you hate this wedding business so much, why did you show up? I'm sure you could have made some excuse to blow it off."

Reed's expression remained impassive. "I might not decorate or plan sunset cocktail parties, but I show up for my friends and lend my support." Julie felt herself soften toward him. Just a little. Then he went and mucked it right up. "I figure when a man is willing to pledge himself to a woman for all eternity, he needs as much support as he can damn well get."

"It's a good thing you're not the best man." She leaned back to study the placement of the lights. "You'd be about as useless as an ashtray on a motorbike."

She thought she heard him chuckle behind her, then decided it was her imagination. "Sorority girls, huh? Let me guess. You were the relentlessly cheerful one in the group.

The do-gooder who forced everyone out of bed, hungover on a Sunday morning, to go perform charity work."

Julie refused to face him when she answered, certain the fact that he'd come uncomfortably close to the truth would show. "Which place of honor did you hold among your friends? Were you the one who pilfered the *Hustler* magazine for all the boys to ogle?"

"Who told you about that?"

"Lucky guess."

Reed made a sound that suggested he didn't believe her. "Anyway, it was a *Penthouse*. July issue."

Julie laughed in surprise, then cut herself off. Her animated laugh had always caused people to look at her strangely. She'd once been told by her Sunday school teacher that she laughed loudly enough to distract Jesus from performing miracles. The gravest of sins, according to the older woman. As a child, she'd taken it to heart and tried to tone down her enthusiastic bursts of amusement, but they often caught her off guard. She cast a look over her shoulder and found Reed watching her with an odd expression on his face. *Great. Something else for him to hold over my head.*

She pinned an arrangement of flowers over where she'd placed the tack and searched for something to fill the sudden silence. "*Penthouse*, huh? Didn't they sell good old-fashioned *Playboy* in Manchester?"

"Sure they did. But a man has to decide what he likes and stick with it."

"And you're one of those men?"

"You already know the answer to that."

Not having heard him move across the room, she felt a jolt of shock when his big hands gripped the backs of her knees. Without warning, heat speared through her and pooled in her belly, tightening every muscle below her waist. Involuntarily, her eyelids fluttered closed and her breathing accelerated. No sound could be heard in the room beyond her pounding heart. It all happened in under five seconds. Rapid, coursing need. How did this man accomplish what no one else ever had?

"W-what are you doing?"

"I need to get to the bottom of something." His thumbs began to massage small circles against her skin and she felt an answering tug in her nipples. "You knew it was me in the dark last night. I need you to admit it, pixie. For my sanity."

Julie said nothing. Tossing and turning in her empty bed last night, she'd admitted as much to herself, but she loathed telling him the truth. Giving him the satisfaction of knowing how easily he could manipulate her body. His ego was big enough. "You're wrong."

He growled. "I'm right."

"We've got ourselves a stalemate." How she managed words was beyond her. Knowing Reed stood behind her, eye level with her bottom, hands wrapped around her legs, did funny things to her brain. "What do we do now?"

"I guess we find out how much higher you want my hands."

Breath escaped her in a rush. "How do we find that out?"

"By being honest."

She started to respond when one hand slipped higher and began kneading the inside of her thigh, just inches from her center, where she'd started to throb painfully in time with his hands. He kept it up for long moments, his big hand working her fevered flesh until she'd started to pant, chest shuddering with each breath. "I have been honest."

His hand stopped moving and she just barely swallowed a whimper of protest. "You see how this is going to work? When you lie, I stop making you feel good." He kneaded her once. "I know you like that. You're giving off so much heat, you're going to burn my hand." She felt his lips at the back of her knee, planting a kiss. "Let's start simple. Do you like what I'm doing right now?"

Julie recognized the moment of truth presenting itself. Did she like it? To say so would be an understatement. She felt like she might burst into flames. His hand, so skilled and capable, sat on her leg unmoving and she wanted to scream at him to keep going. He wanted her to admit she liked it first. Wanted her to admit she'd shamelessly begged him for more of his rough treatment last night in the darkness. Something she'd never done in her life. Especially with a man like Reed. Dark, dangerous...interested in only one thing. Never had a man treated her with anything less than respect. Reed, on the other hand, didn't give a damn about her recognizable last name. Where she came from. Whose names sat on the branches of her family tree.

He wanted to take her to bed. Plain and simple. She had no experience with men like him. Men who took what they wanted and damn the consequences. He represented the unknown, something terrifying for a routine-oriented girl like her. Until now, all her partners had been met through acquaintances after being thoroughly vetted. Or she met them at church on Sunday like most God-fearing Southern girls. She was on her own here. No one to guide her or warn her about the dangers of getting involved with a bad boy. If she wanted this, she could take it. It could be the adventure she'd been secretly wanting for so long. Her chance to cut loose.

But what came after?

"I asked you a question. Do you like the way I'm touching you?"

Don't think about it, Julie. Live in the moment for once. "Yes, I-I like it."

At once, his hand tightened on her thigh almost painfully, then slid a little higher. When the massage started again, he was so close to the barrier of her underwear, she had to bite her lip to keep from moaning. God, the thought of his hand touching her there...she suddenly needed it more than her next breath. Somehow she held her tongue and waited.

"Good. I like it, too. Too damn much." He made a hungry sound. "The second you walked outside last night and let down all that hair, I wanted to fuck you. If you'd stayed any longer, you'd have been gripping the railing, screaming for God. You knew it, too, didn't you?"

Julie gasped as his knuckles brushed over her aching core. "Yes. I knew."

Through her damp panties, he sank a thick knuckle into her opening and twisted. Julie cried out, her hands flying to the rafter in front of her, seeking purchase when her knees threatened to buckle. "When you look at me, baby, do I strike you as the type of man who lets the woman he intends to fuck walk into another man's hotel room?"

"No." Her voice shook. "*No.*"

"That's why you slipped Golden Boy's key into your purse right in front of me with all the subtlety of a high school marching band. You expected me, *wanted* me, to stop you. How am I doing?"

She felt sweat beading her forehead. Legs shaking beneath her, she didn't have the ability to do anything but tell the truth. "I-I kept thinking you'd follow me. Stop me from going inside. When you didn't…I pictured you anyway. Touching me."

"Goddamn right you did," Reed growled, cupping her mound and squeezing. "You thought I'd let someone else touch this? Not a fucking chance."

Cool air washed over her bottom as he lifted her skirt over her hips, leaving her backside completely exposed to him, save her cotton thong. She'd never behaved so provocatively in private, let alone in a public place. As the restaurant didn't open until dinnertime, they were alone in the empty lounge area, but people would be arriving soon to prepare for the evening. The encompassing heat turning her limbs to liquid battled with her ingrained sense of propriety. "Reed, someone might see us. Please…"

"I wouldn't allow anyone to look at you like this." His deeply aroused voice sent a shiver racing up her back. Very slowly, he nudged aside the material of her panties and sank his thumb inside her, pressing firmly against her front inner wall. She gasped at the unexpected pressure, her thighs tightening around his hand reflexively. "No, no. Keep them open. Let me find your spot. I'll be the first to touch it, won't I?" He gave a low groan as he rotated his thumb. "I bet in college you barely ever let anyone under those too-short skirts. Dying for a man, weren't you?"

His thumb brushed over some hidden part of her and with a throaty cry, she nearly toppled from the ladder, but caught herself on the wooden beam at the last second. "*Reed.* I'm…I'm going to fall."

"No. You will *not* fall. You will stay right there until I'm finished." His thumb found the sensitive area again and smoothed over it, once, twice, as if coaxing it to life. Then he began to stroke it rapidly with the pad of his thumb. Julie couldn't form a single thought as the orgasm came hurtling through her system, blasting her with such blissful heat she became unaware of anything but the place Reed made contact with her body. Her head fell forward as she rambled unintelligently, eyes blind as the area between her legs contracted and released over and over again. She felt his teeth sink into the flesh of her ass, then his tongue lick over the spot to soothe the sting.

A door slammed somewhere out in the main dining room. Before Julie could process the sound or what it meant, Reed pulled her off the ladder and tucked her against his chest protectively.

His mouth brushed over her ear. "Think you can stand, baby?"

The teasing hint in his voice stirred her temper. She'd just experienced an exceptionally intense climax. With someone she had no business making time with. Didn't even *like*. And he had the nerve to make jokes. She squirmed out of his embrace and smoothed her dress down over her legs hastily. "Oh, I think I can just about manage. If I swoon, there are smelling salts in my purse."

"A few more minutes on that ladder and they might have been necessary."

"Didn't your mama ever teach you arrogance is a sin?"

"You love the way I sin."

Julie opened her mouth to respond when Christine breezed into the room and came to an almost comical halt, flushing a deeper red than her hair. "Oh. Uh…I just came to see if I could help with the dickorating. I-I mean…decorating. Oh, God. Am I interrupting something?"

Without breaking eye contact with Reed, Julie answered brightly. "You're not interrupting, sweetheart. Mr. Lawson here was just about to take himself off." When Reed's jaw flexed in irritation, Julie smiled, let her gaze drop for a split second to his jeans. She had the sudden urge to put him in his place, throw him off-kilter like he'd so effortlessly done to her. "I'm guessing he needs to go stroke his ego in private for a while," she whispered for his ears alone.

He shook his head once, slowly. "That's a dangerous game you're playing."

Feeling bold, Julie shrugged with indifference. "Yet I appear to be winning. Two to nothing."

"Not for long."

"I guess we'll see."

Reed leaned in so close, his breath fanned across her lips. "Oh, don't worry, pixie. When this week is over, I'll have seen every inch of you."

With a nod in Christine's direction, he turned and left.

Chapter Seven

Reed sat alone in the corner of Spago, animated conversation and scraping silverware creating a noisy void around him as he watched Julie flit about the room, practically sprinkling pixie dust everywhere she went. She hadn't sat down once in the last two hours, nor had she stopped to eat her plate of duck confit salad that still sat untouched at her table. As if salad were a meal. Being in law enforcement, he observed people for a living and he had to admit, he'd never watched someone quite as interesting as Julie. He'd concluded during the earlier cocktail reception that she must possess a built-in mechanism for homing in on guests who were having a less-than-perfect time. Within seconds, she'd have them dazzled with some amusing anecdote, introducing them to another guest with whom they magically seemed to have something in common.

She signaled waiters to refill drinks, straightened tablecloths, and gushed over everyone's outfit, whether or not it was warranted. She listened to boring stories from Colton's grandparents with nothing short of captivated interest on her pretty face. She lowered the music. She turned it back up.

Yet she refused to sit the hell down and *eat* something. For the life of him, Reed could not understand why he cared that she was likely starving. Or that those silver high heels were surely doing a number on her feet. Or if her face was going to crack from all that smiling. It shouldn't make a damn speck of difference to him. Only something continued to bother him about that phone call with her mother he'd overheard this afternoon. The one that had filled her big blue eyes up with tears and made her go pale. *Not everyone can be that perfect,* she'd said. How much more *perfect* could one get? Oh, he knew what lay underneath the bright, shiny surface. He could hardly stand waiting to glimpse it again. But this on-the-surface Julie? He couldn't find one single imperfection. Not one flaw that hinted at the vulnerable girl beneath. Obviously, she felt the need to keep up the illusion of perfection around the clock. He suspected there was more to the reason than simply a desire to decorate and make folks happy.

Damn it if he wasn't impatient to find out the reason. So he could tell her it didn't preclude her from sitting down and letting everyone else fend for themselves for ten goddamn minutes while she ate a plate of fancy lettuce.

Without a single glance in his direction, she slid into the booth behind him where an older couple sat eating braised short ribs. Reed didn't recognize them but he suspected they were related to the bride. He sighed as she launched into another excited greeting wherein he already knew she wouldn't pause for breath once.

"Mr. and Mrs. Wilcox, is that you eating over here all

alone, bless your hearts? I've been looking high and low trying to find you two. Just how big are those grandbabies now? Strapping young men is what they are. I'll tell y'all a secret, they look just like you, Mr. Wilcox, and doesn't that just spell trouble for the young ladies in their class? You best keep an eye on him tonight, Mrs. Wilcox. He's got the look of a smooth operator if I ever laid eyes on one. A plain old fox in a henhouse. Let's get you a refill on that champagne."

By the end of her speech, Reed was massaging his forehead with his thumb and forefinger. How did she do it? Her bubbly energy was inhuman. She'd done her part by decorating the whole damn place, which even Reed had to admit looked pretty damn spiffy. Now she had to go around making sure everyone felt warm and cuddly, too?

Reed slid out of the booth and crossed the room to lean against the bar next to Brock, who sipped his beer pensively as he watched Regan on the other side of the room.

"Seems I might have to make an effort with that one," he said sourly.

"Welcome to my world."

"Blondie causing you trouble?"

Reed grunted as he tipped back the beer the bartender placed in front of him. "I wouldn't call it trouble, so much as an ulcer."

Brock laughed. "Sounds promising."

"I guess we'll see," Reed responded, grimacing as he heard himself repeat Julie's earlier words. He didn't like their ring of uncertainty. It had been a long time since he'd been uncertain of anything. Perhaps it bothered him even more at that very moment, surrounded as he was by some of the only people in the world who knew so much about that uncertain period of his life. When, as a kid, he hadn't known where his next meal would come from. Whether or not he'd make it through to next week. If his father would come up with the rent money gambling, or they'd once again be forced into a shelter until he hit another "lucky" streak.

Brock nudged him with an elbow, dragging him from his dark reverie. He jerked his chin toward a corner of the lounge where large poster boards had been set up, cluttered with pictures of Kady and Colton, encompassing their lives from birth to the present. Staring up at them was Sophie, Colton's little sister and thus, *their* surrogate sister, looking lonely and out of place in workout pants and an oversize T-shirt. Nodding in unspoken agreement, he and Brock made their way toward Sophie, coming up on either side.

She jumped at their sudden appearance, and tugged self-consciously at her shirt. "Oh boy. You guys aren't going to give me a noogie, are you?"

Brock smiled and tapped her on the nose. "Rest assured. I'm on my best behavior. I can't speak to Reed's intentions, mind you."

He felt a smile threaten when Sophie quirked a censorious eyebrow at him. He'd always had a soft spot for the shy, slightly pudgy girl who'd shadowed them during those hot summers in Manchester all those years ago. She'd lost the pudge sometime since he'd last seen her, but the shy had stuck around. Like her brother and Brock, she'd never judged him or made him feel like he didn't belong with the well-raised children. Even though he probably hadn't belonged, despite their assurances. "I ought to noogie you, Miss Sophie. I thought we had a deal. You don't tell anyone about that issue of *Penthouse* and we let you come swimming at the lake on Tuesdays."

Her face broke into a pretty smile. "Haven't you heard of a statute of limitations?"

"Look at you, talking real fancy now," Brock drawled. "Besides, I thought it was a *Hustler*."

"Does it honestly make a difference?" Sophie asked.

"Yes," the men replied emphatically.

Sophie said something else, but Reed became distracted by a picture pinned to the poster board. Front and center stood Kady, wearing a crown in front of a mechanical bull. In the background, looking fresh and innocent, Julie smiled brightly at the camera. Posing in jean shorts and cowboy boots. Long legs dangling on either side of the damn mechanical bull. Without a second thought, Reed reached up and snagged the picture off the board, stuffing it into his jacket pocket. If the sexy photo made him hard, he'd be damned before he left it around to have the same effect on someone else. He felt a prickle move over his neck and turned to find Julie watching him through narrowed eyes, obviously having witnessed his thievery.

He winked at her.

• • •

Julie steadied a tipsy Mr. Wilcox on his feet and waved him out the door. "Now you get back to your room safe, understand? No getting fresh with Mrs. Wilcox in any dark stairwells. There are cameras everywhere now, you know. Eyes in the sky. It's not just the good Lord you have to worry about judging you anymore. These resort folks will call the police faster than you can spit. They don't realize we grow our men friskier in the South, do they, Mrs. Wilcox?

No ma'am, they don't. There you go, one foot in front of the other. You've got the agility of a cougar. Not that kind of cougar, Mrs. Wilcox. Now who's getting fresh?"

The jolly couple disappeared at the end of the hallway, marking the last guests to leave. As soon as they left her field of vision, Julie slumped back against the wall, already reaching down to slip off her high heels. She gave in to the urge to sit right down on the carpeted floor and she ran her thumb up the arch of her foot, moaning at the sheer pleasure.

"Careful, pixie. You keep making those sounds, I might have to join you on that floor."

Julie jolted to her feet as Reed strode through the double doors of the kitchen holding a tray of covered dishes. She hadn't seen him in half an hour and had assumed he left. Had been simultaneously glad and disappointed when she didn't see him reclaim his seat in the darkest corner of the restaurant. Glad, because the heat of his constant regard made it difficult to concentrate. On anything. Disappointed, because the heat felt so darn good. It wrapped itself around her, sliding up and down her thighs, belly, and breasts like a living, breathing thing. Throughout the night, she'd found herself positioning herself where he could see her, lest she lose the heady buzz of his attention for one second. At one point, she'd found herself wishing the room was empty, save herself and Reed, so she could join him where he sat in the dark, straddle his lap and… dance for him. Put those secret lessons she'd been taking to good use in a way he'd probably never see coming. Let him look at her up close while she moved. Feel his penetrating stare trace a path up her writhing midsection. She wanted to open his shirt and look at his tattoos while she performed for him. Since starting the classes, she'd had fantasies about dancing for a man, but he'd never had an identity before. Now, in her mind's eye, Reed looked up at her in awe, lust a living thing on his face.

When Julie realized she hadn't spoken once since Reed's entrance, she shook herself from her fevered thoughts, ignoring the look of amusement on Reed's face. "What are you carrying?"

"Your dinner."

"Pardon?" She slipped her heels back on. "I already ate dinner." Hadn't she?

"No. You didn't. Believe me." He kicked out a chair with his foot, indicating that she should sit. "How can you eat when you never stop talking?"

Julie shoved the chair back under the table. "As opposed to you, who wouldn't say two words if somebody was on fire."

"I'm talking to *you* right now."

"It must be my lucky day."

"All right, fine. You leave me no choice but to play hardball." He kicked the chair out once more. "Back home, when someone goes to the trouble of making you a meal, what is the polite thing to do?"

She gasped.

Reed shook his head. "Where are your manners, pixie?"

Julie sat with a scowl. "Probably poisoned it," she grumbled.

He set the tray down on the table in front of her and lifted lids off three dishes, aromatic steam curling from braised short ribs, honey-glazed salmon, and a side of julienned carrots. Julie's head spun as hunger assailed her, her stomach growling as if it suddenly realized she hadn't eaten since breakfast. She watched as Reed grabbed the fork and took one bite from each plate, raising an eyebrow at her as he chewed. "If it's poisoned, we're both doomed."

"You can't kill the devil."

He smirked. "Eat."

When she took the first bite of perfectly cooked meat, her eyes closed and she stopped caring that Reed sat across from her, watching her every move. The food simply tasted too good on her tongue. Before she could get too full, she set the fork down and leaned back in her chair. "No more. If eat too much, I fall asleep, and I still have to clean this place up.

His face transformed with disbelief. "You've got to be joking."

Sneaking one last carrot off the plate, she shook her head. "No, I really do fall asleep. Right where I stand. Ever since I was a kid."

"I mean, you've got to be joking about cleaning this damn place." He crossed his arms over his chest. "It's after midnight and you're ready to fall on your ass."

"Anyone ever tell you that you've got a way with words?"

He sighed loudly. Julie watched in curiosity as a battle took place on his face. As if he wanted to wash his hands of the whole situation, but couldn't bring himself to do it. *How odd.* "No."

She straightened. "*No?*"

"Someone else is going to clean this shit up. And it ain't you." Reed took her hand and pulled Julie to her feet. "Come on. We're going for a walk. I'm tired of being cooped up indoors."

"Why do you have to drag me along with you?"

"If I leave you here, you'll clean," he explained, then came to a stop, glancing down at her feet. "You bring some decent sneakers along, or just those medieval torture devices disguised as shoes?"

Chapter Eight

Julie followed Reed on the dark path leading up the side of the mountain. He'd brought a flashlight with him, but so far it had proved unnecessary, the full moon providing more than enough illumination to see where they walked through the trees. He'd run this path that very morning and had memorized it easily. He knew exactly where he wanted to take her. Did she know what his intentions were? He'd made no secret about wanting her. The possibility that she'd come with him in the middle of the night, hoping for the same outcome, heated his blood.

He cast a look over his shoulder, sighing inwardly when he glimpsed her expression. Too bad she looked scared half to death. She might want him, but the situation clearly made her more than a little nervous. Hell, *he* obviously made her a little nervous. Not a good thing. And entirely his fault. He'd never been one to hold back in the bedroom, physically or verbally, but he'd laid it on extra thick with Julie, playing a game of "shock the snooty rich girl." To show her that he was nothing like the old-money, loafer-wearing pretty boys he suspected she usually dated.

Now it had backfired. After all the ways he'd provoked and taunted her, she'd placed her trust in him and gone out with him into the woods, the expectation being that they would finally slake this insane attraction between them. Only now it didn't feel right. He didn't want her nervous or questioning her judgment. He wanted her to feel...confident in him. Instead, she appeared seconds from turning tail and booking it back to the resort. It bothered him. A lot more than it should.

Hell. It wasn't going to happen between them tonight.

Reed practically growled into the darkness. When the hell had he ever cared about being noble? She was a big girl, capable of making her own decisions. Yet he suspected if they slept together tonight, she would regret it in the morning. They barely knew each other. Their only association so far had been him making passes at her at every opportunity and arguing. She'd wake up tomorrow, a little sore and a lot sorry. For some reason, he couldn't stand the thought of it. Gratification tonight wouldn't be worth having her look back on him with regret. As the stranger she'd had a hot, sweaty one-night stand with, the one who had nothing in common with her. She would feel cheap and she would associate that feeling with him. No. He couldn't do it.

Decision made, he figured it wouldn't hurt to find out just a little more about her. They might part ways at the end of the week, but small talk had never actually *killed* anyone, right? Besides, he'd been curious about something since he first laid eyes on her. "Last night, when we met outside the restaurant, you looked stressed. Mind telling me what about?"

She moved beside him on the path, flashing him a look. "When you made your gentlemanly hair-pulling offer? I nearly fainted dead away at the sweeping romance of it all."

"I would have caught you. By the hair, of course." He circled his hand around her wrist, then fit their hands together as if it were natural for him to do so. It wasn't, but he felt the ridiculous urge to put her at ease. "Still waiting on an answer."

Julie merely sighed. "A work meeting that morning had made me late for my flight. There was a big"—she waved her free hand around as she searched for the right word—"*hullabaloo* over whether or not we should offer One-Eyed Jack at the New Orleans Saints stadium. You know, in those fancy air-conditioned suites? I'm sure you know the Saints are the biggest rivals of our dearly beloved Falcons, and Daddy doesn't want our whiskey anywhere near them. No, sir. Thinks it'll put a jinx on the Falcons."

Reed hid his shock. He'd known Julie came from money, but the heir to One-Eyed Jack Whiskey? Holy shit. He'd had no idea. Not that it changed a damn thing. "And how did you manage to straighten out this little *hullabaloo*?"

She smirked at him. "I told Daddy I'd have him committed if he fought me on it. Can you imagine? Superstition has no place in the business world."

"I thought all Southern girls were superstitious."

"Oh, I am. Within reason. I would never invite thirteen guests to a dinner party. Or eat chicken on New Year's Day. It's just plain silly to tempt fate."

"I see." Reed realized he was smiling and shook his head

to clear it. "So who is Serena?"

When her hand went stiff in his, he wanted to kick himself. Based on the phone call he'd overheard, he knew the subject was likely a touchy one. *This* is why he never made small talk. They walked in silence for a moment, then she turned to him with a smile that didn't reach her eyes. "Serena was my older sister. She passed a few years back."

"I'm sorry."

She nodded in acknowledgment as if she'd heard the words so many times they no longer held any meaning. He understood that too well. Growing up, he'd heard the same words countless times in reference to his own mother. After she'd died, he couldn't go anywhere without having pity leveled at him from every direction, from people who'd never given him the time of day before. When the appropriate time limit for grief over her death had passed, they'd begun issuing "sorrys" for different things, as if the pity were transferable. They were sorry about his shabby lifestyle, living in a trailer on the outskirts of town. Sorry about his father's gambling habit. Everything under the sun. *Sorry, boy*. Again, he recalled Julie's words to her mother. The way she'd sounded so dejected as she'd spoken them, as if it were far from the first time. "If Serena was the perfect one, what does that make you?"

Julie kept walking, but the action looked involuntary. As if her legs were moving without her permission. "I think you're aware I didn't come out here with you for a heart-to-heart. Stop trying to make this personal. We're not friends."

Maybe that's the problem. Reed banished the unbidden thought as quickly as it appeared. This desire to peel back her layers, to figure out what made her run like the Energizer

Bunny, unnerved and confused him. "You came out here with me knowing how badly I want to be inside you. There's nothing more personal than that." *Jesus. Since when?*

She came to a stop, studied him. Her mask slipped just a little and he felt an answering tug in his chest. "Fine. Tell me how you got that horrible scar on your back and I'll tell you why Serena was the perfect one. The one who never let my parents down. The one who was supposed to take over the business when Daddy retired. The one who died while I was off at college planning Hawaiian-themed dances and ice cream socials."

Julie's mouth snapped shut when she finished, as if she couldn't believe what she'd revealed. When she turned and stomped off ahead of him, Reed quickly followed. Part of him wished for all the world he hadn't pushed her. The other part, the greedy half, felt satisfaction over being privy to this hidden part of her. She didn't put on her Princess of Hospitality act around him, didn't hide her true self. Later, he'd try to figure out why, but right now all he could think of was taking the haunted expression off of her face. Unfortunately, in order to do that, he would have to reveal a part of himself to make them even.

"Bar fight."

"Pardon?"

"The scar. I got knifed in a bar fight when I was nineteen." She stopped and turned, meeting his eyes hesitantly. He hadn't told anyone about the fight in a long time and suddenly the words wouldn't come quite so easy. "I, uh…had started a fight in the bar over God knows what. It spilled out into the alley. Next thing I knew there were five of them." He shrugged. "They were young and stupid like me. Didn't realize what they were doing…so they left me there bleeding and ran off."

Her gaze caressed his shoulder. "That's an awful story."

"Maybe. It's also the best thing that ever happened to me." He crossed his arms over his chest. "I almost didn't make it that night. Lost too much blood. I applied to the academy the day I was released from the hospital. If I have to die, I want there to be a purpose behind it."

Julie looked at him in awe. "This has to be the least romantic moonlight walk in the history of moonlight walks, you know that?"

"Hate to disappoint, but I don't have a romantic bone in my body."

"You don't say." She sighed. "I know you were trying to make me feel better and it worked."

"Because you like the idea of me getting stabbed?"

"No, even I'm not that bloodthirsty." She tilted her head. "Because if you'll tell that terrible story just to make me feel better, then you're not half as bad as I thought."

"I'm worse."

She smiled, but it faded almost immediately. "Reed, I appreciate what you're trying to do, but I don't understand it either. We're…attracted to each other. I won't deny that. But I think we both known that is the extent of what we have in common. Let's not make this something it isn't."

An odd feeling crept over him. He didn't recognize it, even though her words had a ring of familiarity. Probably because he was usually the one to say them. To someone else. She wanted him for sex and nothing else. He should be backing her against a tree. Instead, he felt more determined than ever to prove her wrong.

...

Julie looked up into Reed's face, confused by what she saw there. Irritation, conflict, and surprise all took their turn passing over his hard yet intensely handsome features until she nearly got dizzy trying to keep up. She'd actually mustered the courage to follow this potty-mouthed, tattooed stab wound recipient into the dark woods and now he refused to just put the darn moves on her already. Once he touched her, once their mouths met, she wouldn't have any room to think. She required the distraction from her thoughts. Didn't want to think of all the reasons she should be tucked safely in her hotel bed, eye mask firmly in place.

For one, she'd never had sex for the sake of sex. Usually, basic fondness or even genuine romantic interest was involved. How did one behave after a one-night stand? A handshake? An email address swap?

Two, she could easily be a big fat disappointment to him. She could count her partners on one hand and Reed… she suspected there weren't enough hands at Beaver Creek Resort to match that impressive number.

Third, she was starting to understand him a little and that simply couldn't happen. She didn't want to feel anything for this man. He would chew up her good-girl butt and spit it out. Heck, he'd already bitten her there once, hadn't he? Hard, too. Absentmindedly, she rubbed the spot on her bottom where he'd bitten her earlier, stopping when Reed arched an eyebrow.

After what seemed like ages, he finally spoke, his gruff tone startling her. "Let me get this straight. You want to skip the small talk and get right to the good stuff?"

She raised her chin, refusing to give in to the urge to turn around and bolt for the hotel. Instead, she inched closer. "I've been making small talk all night. I'm ready for something…else. Are you the one who's going to give it to me or not?"

A muscle ticked in his jaw. "Normally, pixie, I wouldn't hesitate to give you a nice, thorough pounding for challenging me like that. God knows, we both need it." He swept her head to toe in a single hot glance. "But it's not going to happen. Not tonight, at least."

Her feminine pride took a nosedive. "What did you haul me out here for in the middle of the night? I thought this is what you wanted."

"You've had me hard for days, baby. I want to fuck you more than I want to breathe."

Scorching heat bathed her head to toe. She tried not to make it obvious when she squeezed her knees closer together. Something, anything to alleviate the ache he'd initiated. But wouldn't fulfill? It made no sense. "Then I-I fail to see the problem. I came out here with you, despite my better judgment—"

"There." Reed jabbed a blunt finger in her direction. "Despite your better judgment. Of me. *That's* the problem."

With a confused frown, Julie opened her mouth to question him further, but he cursed and took her arm, leading her into the wooded area, off the beaten path. Mulling over his words in silence, Julie followed behind him for a few minutes before he came to an abrupt stop. A few feet in front of them, what looked like a small pond was nestled among the trees. Soft light filtered through the branches and illuminated the surface, giving it an almost ethereal look. Combined with the soft sounds of the woods and the warm breeze sifting through the trees, the scene before her could only be described as breathtaking.

Their odd conversation forgotten for the moment, she felt Reed's gaze on her and turned. "What is this place? How did you know it was here?"

He shrugged, but didn't look at her. "Went for a run this morning and found it. It's a hot spring."

As he stared off at some invisible point in the distance, Julie studied his strong profile closely. Proud, stubborn, strong...gorgeous man. And evidently, thoughtful. Whatever his motive, the front-runner being taking her to bed, Reed had *thought* about her tonight. Made sure she ate a hot dinner. Brought her to this beautiful spot for her enjoyment. She'd wounded his pride by referring to him as a lapse in judgment. Although he would probably wear a blond wig and a push-up bra before admitting it out loud. Julie couldn't stop the laugh that tickled her throat at the image and only laughed harder when Reed shot her a suspicious glance.

"Something funny?"

With a sigh, Julie slowly shook her head. Her nervous energy had completely fled, she realized. She felt...good, safe, being here with Reed. Unfortunately, by taking sex off the table, he'd only presented her with a challenge. She'd never been able to resist a challenge. And first impressions aside, she wanted him. It wouldn't go away until she did something about it. Prying her hands from her elbows, Julie reached for the hem of her dress. Heck, she was from the South. She'd gone skinny-dipping before. Seen all ten of her male cousins naked as you please every summer until they all hit puberty one by one. This was an entirely different situation, however. The man watching her with a predatory gleam in his eye, looking so at home surrounded by nature it could be his natural habitat, wasn't interested in playing Marco Polo.

You made it this far, Julie. Hop to. He's already seen your butt and he seemed to like it just fine. And if you have to get naked in front of a man, this is the best lighting you could ever hope for. Strip.

Before she could talk herself out of it, she tugged her dress over her head and kicked off her sandals, as if it were the most natural thing in the world.

"What the hell are you doing?" His raw, slightly startled tone thrilled her, heated her further. She'd surprised him. Good.

When her hands went to unhook her bra at the back, she thought she heard him groan but wouldn't allow herself any hesitation to find out. The panties came next, tossed onto the pile with the rest of her clothes.

As Julie waded into the water, she cast what she hoped was a sultry look over her shoulder. "Are you going to stand there and look all night?" Strategically, she bit her lip, ran her hands over her hips. "Or are you going to come in here and make yourself useful?"

She sank into the divinely warm water and closed her eyes, focusing on the gentle breeze and night sounds, hoping to take her mind off the possibility that Reed wouldn't take her not-so-subtle bait. A moment later, when she heard his pants and belt hit the ground, she turned away so he wouldn't see her victorious grin, but she couldn't resist looking back to see him in the nude.

Really, it was only fair after she'd given him a close-up of her birthday suit.

Moonlight spilled over his muscular stomach and thighs, so sleek and toned she could do nothing but shake her head as he entered the spring. His long, thick erection demanded her attention next, had her catching her breath on a shudder. She felt a brief resurgence of nerves, but pushed them aside. Her choice. She'd initiated this. Determinedly, she dragged her gaze up his impressive chest to meet hard, lust-filled eyes.

"I don't say anything without a reason." Submerged now past his waist, he stalked her. "Once my mind has been made up, it doesn't change."

His hypnotic voice vibrated inside her, his deliberate movements battering her with their sensuality. With a mental shake, she tried to focus on his words. When he moved within reaching distance, she inhaled deeply for courage and rose to her full height, causing water to course down her breasts and belly. She ran her hands over his chest and let their damp bodies meet, looked up at him through her eyelashes. "Aren't you even going to let me try?"

His head dipped toward hers, and he nipped at her bottom lip with a growl. "No. Enough questioning. We both take some relief tonight, but not all of it." A rough hand smoothed over her bottom, gave it a light slap. "You'll know the difference when I fuck you."

Reed's mouth descended on hers. His fists tangled in her hair and angled her head so he could kiss her hard, tongue sweeping in to claim absolute possession. Julie clung to his wide, slippery shoulders and lost herself in the kiss, moaning as heat slammed through her in pounding waves. She'd been frantic for the taste of him without even realizing just how much. Now, she made up for the achy, restless feeling she'd been cursed with all day and took, took, *took*. He growled when her fingers slid up into his hair and tugged, her body pressing flush against his simultaneously. Reed fit his hips against the notch between her thighs and surged up, creating a wave around them. With each strategic push, Julie's throaty cries echoed through the night.

"Do you hurt between your legs, baby?"

"Yes," she sobbed, writhing on his lap, frustrated by the water hindering her movements. "Reed, please don't make me wait. It hurts so badly."

"Who made it hurt?"

"You know you did," she whispered.

"Ask me." He sucked her bottom lip into his mouth. "Ask me to take away the pain."

Julie groaned. "Take it *away*." Before the words fully left her mouth, Reed lifted her out of the water, her bare bottom slapping down onto the edge of the smooth rock bed surrounding the spring. His hands gripped her knees and pushed them wide, shoulders wedging between her legs to keep them open as he licked his way up the inside of her thighs.

"You're only getting tongue tonight, pixie," he rasped, his breath heating her damp skin. "Your pussy is going to have to wait a little longer to be filled."

"No," she moaned, even as she mentally begged for his mouth to make contact. Anything. She just needed *something* to ease the rapidly growing need. When seconds passed and Reed still didn't follow through on his sensual threat, Julie realized he'd stopped kissing her completely. She opened her eyes to find him staring down at her thighs, helpless anger blanketing his features.

"What are these bruises?" He looked into her eyes. "Who did this to you?" His urgent words confused her for a few seconds, then recognition dawned, followed quickly by mortification. She tried to sit up, but he put a hand on her belly to stay her. "Answer me."

Her hands came up to hide her face. Of course. This would only happen to her. Two seconds from the most amazing sexual experience of her life, in a moonlit forest, with a man who embodied every woman's darkest, most secret fantasy, and now she was being forced to reveal something she'd hoped to take with her to the grave. "Ms. Vaughn. She gave them to me. This is all her fault."

Reed made an impatient noise when she didn't continue. "I'm waiting."

"Pole dancing," she blurted. "They're from pole dancing. Not on a stage, mind you. It's a class at the gym, you see. I thought I'd signed up for cardio kickboxing, but when I walked in, I found sweet Ms. Vaughn, an honest, churchgoing woman if I ever met one, standing there next to a pole. Pretty as you please. She looked so excited that somebody actually showed up, I just couldn't turn around and walk out. By the end of the hour, she'd signed me up for an eight-class package." Julie peeked up at him through her fingers. "Now...I think I kind of like it," she whispered.

For long moments, he only stared at her in disbelief. Then his big body began to shake with laughter. It sounded surprised at first, but it quickly turned pained.

"Just what are you laughing at, Reed Lawson?" She sat up and poked him in the chest. "I'm darned impressive on that thing. Last week I learned the Bendy Diva Dive. Do you know how difficult that is? You have to—"

"Stop. Stop right there." He pressed a finger to her lips, then sighed over her still-disgruntled expression. "Baby, if I don't laugh, I'll cry."

She shook her head. "I don't understand you."

Reed took her mouth in a slow, thorough kiss. Tongues met and savored. Lust, simmering and desperate, once again chased the anger from her body. He pulled back to speak against her parted lips. "The only thing you need to understand right now is the way my mouth makes you feel *here*." Julie gasped as he penetrated her with two thick fingers, slid them in and out, pushing deeper each time. "You spent the whole night making everyone else happy. Now I'm going to use my tongue to reward you for it. Be selfish for a little while, pixie. God knows I'm selfish to get a taste."

He gave her a gentle push and she fell back, moaning when his fingers began to stroke her faster. Julie closed her eyes and let sensation take over. When his middle finger crooked and rotated, finding that delicious spot inside her, her back arched on a cry. She felt the heat of his mouth between her thighs. He flicked her aching clitoris with his tongue, in perfect rhythm with his pumping fingers. Julie could feel her sex begin to clench, the heat within her rising to a boiling point. Reed's fingers moved faster, in and out, urging her closer. Dangling over the edge, she felt him suck her clitoris into his mouth, rolling it on his tongue and growling. His fingers pushed deep and held. Julie screamed as the orgasm rushed through her, legs and stomach shaking, but even then Reed refused to stop. Seemed as though he *couldn't* stop.

"Again." He dragged his tongue up her center, causing

her already-sensitive flesh to contract and spasm. "Want more. Again."

Julie's limbs felt liquefied and the thought of lying back and letting Reed's mouth work another blistering climax out of her sounded like absolute perfection. But her firmly ingrained need to please simply wouldn't allow it. Before she'd consciously made the decision, she'd sat up and tugged his head from where he'd tucked it between her thighs. When his gaze met hers, he looked just as delirious with pleasure as she felt, but it couldn't be possible. She'd done nothing for him, yet his erection, thick and heavy against her thigh, told her how badly he needed her to reciprocate.

She gave in to the temptation to lean forward and kiss his wet, muscular chest as her hand moved of its own accord to wrap him in her fist. The second she touched him, he let out a loud groan, hips driving forward to be stroked in her palm. "Squeeze it tight, baby. Show me how it'll feel when I fuck you between your legs."

Julie whimpered, a new, intense throb forming low in her belly. The kind that could only be assuaged by one thing. "Why don't you just find out right now?"

Reed growled. "That's how it's going to be." He yanked her to the very end of the rock bed by her knees, then his hands slipped up her belly to palm her breasts. When he rolled her nipples between his thumb and forefinger, her thighs pressed together tightly in response. It felt like a snapping live wire ran directly from her breasts to her core. "You weren't wearing a bra underneath your dress that first night. Every time you moved, they bounced a little. Just enough to be a hot fucking tease. God, baby, it made my cock hard."

Her breath rushed in and out past her lips. To know she'd turned him on, fully clothed in a room full of people, made her feel outrageously sexy. Something she wasn't familiar with. People tended to view her as the one who ran the show. The tireless, unflappable one who dressed stylishly, yet sensibly. Oh boy, she liked this sense of desirability much, *much* better. It made her feel daring. Powerful. Combined with the near-darkness and unconventional setting, it also made her just a little crazy for more.

"How about I make it up to you?" Before she could stop herself she slid his erection onto her damp chest. Then she pressed her breasts tight around him, trapping him in between the supple flesh.

Reed's breath grew choppy, scraping over her heightened senses. One hand gripped her head and tilted it back roughly so their gazes could meet. "I ought to put you over my knee." His eyes were nearly hidden by the darkness, but she somehow sensed they were burning into hers. "You want me to despoil you? I hope you're ready, because I don't fuck politely."

"I'm counting on it," she answered breathily.

He slid himself upward between her breasts, in one long, slow push. Julie moaned quietly at the illicitness of it, but Reed drowned out the sound with his own wild groan. Their position, the new experience, the delicious feeling of his smooth flesh slipping through her breasts, intoxicated her. Her usual self didn't seem present any longer. Had been replaced by someone else entirely. Someone whose every thought was driven by feeling. Taking and giving.

As his movements became faster, impatient, Julie reveled in the harsh sounds emanating from his throat, the way he swelled larger with each measured drive. She pushed her breasts tighter around him and whispered his name.

His movements stuttered and he looked down at her hard. "Open your mouth. You want my name on your tongue, you'll get the rest of me, too."

Julie suddenly couldn't think past taking Reed into her mouth. Closing her lips around him, feeling his weight. She dragged her nails down his belly and grasped him at the base of his erection, then led him to her mouth. No teasing, or licking, she took him as deep as she could and swirled her tongue over his hardness on the way back up. Fingers sank into her hair and she heard him shouting harshly in the distance, but she'd lost herself in the need to please. Her hand worked him in time with her mouth and when she felt him coat her tongue, shaking against her in his climax, she continued milking him until he gently tugged her head away and fell back a step in the water.

"Jesus. *Jesus*, baby." Reed's chest rose and fell rapidly as he tried to catch his breath. Julie didn't stop to question herself. She went to him, arms cinching around his waist to bring them closer. He seemed unsure of how to proceed, his muscles tensing beneath her, making her throat close. She was the sole participant in the hug, his arms never coming up to encircle her like she craved. Her brain commanded her to pull back but she didn't want the embarrassment on her face to show. Not over what they'd done, but over her spontaneous embracing of a man who had all the sweetness of a cobra.

And then he laughed uncomfortably. "I guess we know that mouth is good at more than just talking."

Julie released him and was out of the hot spring in

seconds, pulling on her clothes as the words continued to hang in the air. *That's* all he could think to say to her? Anger had a stranglehold on her throat so tight she couldn't speak past it. What had she been thinking? This man couldn't even muster a decent hug for the woman he'd just been intimate with. She didn't want to spend one more second in his presence. Julie was also honest enough to admit that maybe, just a little, she was shaken up by the way she'd lost herself in him so completely.

His dripping hand closed around her arm as she buckled her sandals. "You hold on one damn minute. I was making a joke and you know it." His voice boomed in the still, quiet forest. "What is this really about? You want me to hold you and tell you you're pretty? That's not me, Julie, and I think you already knew that."

"The only thing I know is this won't be happening again."

"Now, that'd be a damn shame, pixie." He tipped her chin up with his fingers. "You just fucking burned me alive."

The air left Julie's lungs. She struggled to come up with a reply as her brain projected explicit images of them together. God, why did she still want him?

He must have sensed her resolve slipping, because his fingers left her chin to slip into her hair, gripping the strands firmly. "You already want more, don't you? You know that what I give you is better than the warm, fuzzy bullshit you're used to."

His bluntness slapped her across the face, as did her resurgence of need to get away from him. "Well, I suppose we'll have to savor this one memory. We're not making any more." She double-checked that her hotel key was still tucked securely into her dress pocket before snatching the flashlight off the ground and striding toward the path.

"You're not walking back alone."

"Watch me."

Julie heard him growl behind her as he pulled on his own clothes. She increased her pace, practically running by the time she reached the hotel. As she yanked the door open, she turned and saw him coming down the path, shirt untucked, hair a mess. Barefoot. Why that made her want to smile, especially after his cold treatment of her, she had no idea. Ignoring the object of her irritation, she let the door slam behind her and speed-walked to her room. How her body could feel so satisfied when her mind felt like it had been pulled through a knothole backwards, she couldn't fathom.

One thing she knew for certain? It was Reed Lawson's fault and she needed to remember this hinky feeling the next time his big shadow darkened her path. The man was flat-out dangerous for her sanity. No more. This ill-advised association was over.

Chapter Nine

His and Julie's association was *far* from over.

Reed crossed his arms over his chest and leaned back against the brick building. He'd given up on sleep sometime around four in the morning and had decided to make himself useful. He still couldn't believe *how* he'd gone about making himself useful, but it was too late to change it now.

Irritation rumbling in his throat, Reed dragged a hand down his face. He had a serious problem and the crisp mountain air was doing precious little to fix it. How exactly had he managed to fuck up a chance to spend the week in Julie's bed? On the surface, the answer was deceptively simple. He'd opened his mouth and let the worst possible post-orgasm sentiment known to man escape. Truthfully, though? He still wasn't 100 percent sure he hadn't done it on purpose. She'd thrown him for a goddamn loop, going from skittish good girl to a heck-I'll-try-*anything*-once sex goddess in mere minutes.

The girl he'd assumed to be an uptight Georgia debutante took regular pole dancing classes. *Enjoyed* them. If he ever got the image of those legs wrapped around a pole out of his head, he might have the chance to register surprise.

Lord, the things they'd done. Things *she'd* initiated. He'd never, ever, expected it from her. And damn it if that wasn't what made it so fucking hot. Everyone's favorite, lovable Goody Two-Shoes turned into a very bad girl under the right kind of touch. *His* touch, specifically. The thought made the ever-present fire in his belly burn brighter, even as he reminded himself how dangerous that type of thinking could be. He didn't have a claim on her. He didn't want or need any emotional entanglements, especially with some upper-class daddy's girl with a wardrobe that likely cost more than his car. Yet the thought of unleashing all her pent-up sensuality, coaxing it to life, then walking away at the end of the week made him…oddly anxious. Okay, sickeningly so.

When his intention had been simply to get under her skirt, stamp an expiration date on the outrageous attraction he felt for her, everything had been so incredibly simple. Show the spoiled, uptight brat what real passion felt like and walk away without a single regret. Someone hadn't passed the memo on to Julie, however. Or maybe *she'd* gotten it, and *he'd* decided to ignore it instead. Now that he knew what lay underneath the top coat of perfect polish, he saw way too much when he looked at her. As if one glimpse at the Julie beneath now made it impossible for him to see the other one.

Yet after what they'd done together, to each other's bodies, she'd turned right back into the vulnerable girl she'd been walking into the forest. She'd wrapped her arms around him and he'd...felt something. Right before panic set in.

He didn't cuddle or reassure. He didn't dole out sweet nothings. He didn't get close to women, or anyone for that matter, save his two closest friends. And it would be a cold day in hell before he whispered sweet nothings in one of *their* ears. Even after such a short acquaintance, he sensed Julie knew this about him. So why she'd gone and *hugged* him, held on to him tightly as if she wanted to absorb him, Reed couldn't guess. He supposed his panic stemmed from the fact that he'd *liked* her arms around him. He'd wanted to gather her up against his chest and sink back into the water. Let them both recover for a while as they drifted. God knows, he'd needed a damn minute after what she'd done to him. He still hadn't completely recovered.

Instead, he'd recognized the dangers of giving in to the urge. This insanity between them needed to find a way to remain casual. To begin with, they were far too different. He didn't even say the word "relationship" out loud. Julie, being less experienced than him, could easily mistake sex for something more. She would start expecting things from him. Things he didn't have a hope in hell of getting right. Growing up, he'd had no example to go by. His parents had been enemies right up until the point his mother died. Even before she'd been diagnosed with cancer, she'd simply been a shell. Made that way from constant criticism—a product of his father's alcohol-fueled hatred. No. It would be up to him to make sure he and Julie didn't go any further than casual. It would only lead to disappointment. *He* would only lead to disappointment, because that was all he'd ever learned how to deliver. It was in his blood. Just look at how he'd gone and offended her two seconds after...

Jesus, after what she'd done with her mouth.

Why then did he wish like hell he could go back in time and pull her closer in that spring?

One thing he harbored zero doubts about? The week wouldn't go by without him having Julie again. Even now, he wanted to go pound on her door and demand to be let in. If luck was on his side, she slept naked so he'd have nothing to stop him from fucking her where she stood.

He shook himself when he saw Brock approaching, looking *nearly* as frustrated as he felt.

"What the hell are you doing up this early?"

Reed raised an eyebrow at Brock's tone, so different from his usual teasing drawl. "I could ask you the same question."

"Well, keep it to yourself, because I haven't got a damn answer."

"I could hazard a guess."

"Same goes." Brock practically threw his body against the wall to join Reed. "You reckon there's something in the water in Colorado that only the women are drinking?"

He cleared his throat, the words "in the water" hitting a little too close to home after his and Julie's episode at the hot springs mere hours ago. "Could be the altitude."

"Altitude," Brock snorted. "More like *attitude*. Let me tell you, I've been getting more than my fair share of that."

"Told you she was trouble."

"Trouble is a significant underestimation."

Reed glanced at Brock in surprise. "Did you swallow a dictionary last night?"

Brock looked affronted. "I can use words longer than one syllable when I put my mind to it. When did everyone start thinking the opposite?"

"You mean, when did you start giving a shit?"

"That, too."

Reed shrugged. "Maybe it's the altitude."

. . .

Julie mounted the treadmill and tightened her ponytail so hard she winced. Her fingers stabbed the buttons, entering a punishing pace and time for herself to contend with. Good. She needed her butt good and kicked. Maybe if she'd had the foresight to work out yesterday morning, she wouldn't have been so tense she lit up like a Christmas tree around Reed Lawson.

The smug, irreverent son of a—

No. Her speed-walk sped up into a run. She wouldn't let one albeit incredible night with Reed turn her into an irritable, insulting person like him. That simply would not do. She'd followed him into the woods like a lamb to slaughter, planning on ridding herself of the inconvenient yen he'd plagued her with. It was her own stupid fault if she'd expected him to soften up a little afterward. They hadn't even had sex, but it certainly felt like they'd been as intimate as two people could be. Her inexperience must have been glaring. Hugging the man as though he were the only shelter in a storm. After only reaching third base.

Honestly, Julie.

Truth was, she didn't reveal her grief and vulnerability regarding her sister to many people. Hated the idea of someone taking pity on her. She'd dealt with enough of that after Serena's death. Perhaps his response had been abrupt, slightly harsh, possibly inappropriate, but at the very least it had been honest. *If Serena was the perfect one, what does that make you?* She suspected Reed had no clue how squarely on the head he'd hammered her biggest insecurity. The very same question she'd asked herself throughout her life. One she didn't have an answer to. For a brief moment, she'd felt as if he could see her. See the horrible guilt and vulnerability she usually kept hidden so well underneath a mask of perpetual perkiness.

Sometimes the burden of it felt like concrete blocks on her shoulders. As the younger sister by five years, she'd grown up abhorring responsibility. Assuming Serena would handle anything and everything like she always did. Without complaint. Julie had flitted off to college with visions of toga parties dancing in her head, leaving her sister with the mighty tasks of catering to their parents' constant whims, running various charities, learning the family business. Julie had never even given it a second thought. She'd wanted to *discover* herself, as far away from Georgia as she could reasonably get.

The single time Serena decided to blow off her responsibilities and go water-skiing with her friends at the lake, she didn't make it home. Her sister had always gone out of her way to help people. Make them feel important. Loved. So when her sister had left a bonfire to retrieve her sweater from a friend's docked boat and slipped and hit her head on the dock, why had no one gone to check on her for over an hour?

None of it was fair. None it made sense. If anyone deserved to pay for being selfish and irresponsible, it had been *Julie*. Not her sister.

Why wasn't it me?

She'd spent four years of her life trying furiously to make up for it, all the while knowing nothing she did could take away the emptiness that went along with every thought of Serena. Her mother grieved to this day, wearing black and carrying around a picture of Serena with her, tucked into her handbag. Julie didn't blame her. How could she? But she'd be lying if she said it didn't weigh on her heart. Watching her mother break down every year when the anniversary of Serena's death rolled around, seeing her father flounder helplessly with no idea how to comfort his wife, ensured that the pain remained fresh.

Last night, she'd revealed a major part of herself, the pain of losing her sister, to Reed. Combined with the intensity of their physical encounter, she'd felt close to him, even if just for the moment. So she'd reached out for him afterward, assuming he felt it, too.

Wrong.

If he came on to her again, she needed to remember how she'd felt when he shattered the notion that they were connected in any way. Yes, they'd been engaging in a temporary fling, but his words had been crude and uncalled for. She'd been hurt by them. Not an acceptable reaction when she'd gone into the encounter expecting only sex.

Now if she could just stop thinking about the way he'd touched her and every deliciously naughty word that had come out of his mouth, she'd be in *excellent* shape. Or maybe if this yearning, unfulfilled feeling would go away, which she suspected was a product of him refusing to put himself inside of her. Julie groaned and squeezed her eyes shut, trying to focus on the pounding rhythm of her feet on the treadmill.

"Should have known you'd be up early, putting all us regular humans to shame."

Julie opened her eyes to the sound of Regan's voice. "It's not early if you never went to sleep in the first place."

"Word of advice?" Regan climbed onto the treadmill beside her. "When insomnia strikes, drink till you pass out."

She laughed in spite of herself. "How are you handling running with a hangover?"

"I guess we'll find out." Regan started to jog. "I've got to do something to work off this excess energy. My libido is running like a hamster on one of those little wheels."

"There's a picture." Julie increased her pace. "Care to share who's got your hamster all worked up?"

"Dropping the hamster reference now."

"You started it."

"Guilty." Regan punched a button and broke into a run. "I'm not worked up, per se. Just a little itchy when I shouldn't be. Know what I mean?"

"Too well, actually."

"Oh! Really? Do tell."

Julie's pace faltered, suspicious gaze swinging toward Regan. Something about her tone was deceptively innocent. No one had ever accused Regan of being innocent. "Why don't you start with the telling? You're acting like a toddler with pudding on his face."

"Please, Julie. Please, speak English. It's way too early for me to translate Southern." She sighed loudly, adding under her breath, "And I've heard way too much of that accent lately."

"It's a musical accent." Julie nudged Regan in the arm. "I'm waiting for an explanation of your tone. You didn't sound quite as sympathetic over my itchiness."

"If someone walked in on this conversation, they would be seriously confused." Regan sent her a sly smile. "I guess I was just wondering why Reed hasn't gotten around to scratching your itch yet."

Julie veered to the side, then righted herself. "How'd you know about Reed? Has he…has he been talking about it?"

"About what?"

"*Regan.*"

She rolled her eyes. "No, he hasn't been talking about it, goober. Anyone who was in the same room with you and Reed that first night knows. You guys were two seconds away from wild, oh-God-I-think-I-see-Jesus sex."

Julie lifted her chin. "I was talking to Logan the whole time."

"Yes, but you were communicating with Reed in every way that counted. A little nudge was all you needed." A flash of uncertainty crossed Regan's face. "Right?"

Julie smacked the stop button and the treadmill screeched to a halt. "*You* switched the keys, didn't you? I should have known. I assumed this whole time it was Reed."

"He sure as shit didn't protest."

Her body reacted instantaneously, which angered Julie even more than Regan taking matters of her love life into her own hands. "Of course he didn't. He has the manners of a tomcat on Sunday."

"You're going Southern on me again." Julie punched a button and started an all-out sprint that had Regan raising her eyebrows. "Uh-oh. She's madder than a wet hen."

"Now who's going Southern?"

Regan gave a firm shake of her head. "Correction. I've

gone Southern. Now I'm going West. It's like my own sexual version of the Gold Rush."

"Panning for orgasms."

"Couldn't have put it better myself."

Half an hour later, Julie shoved open the door of Spago and checked her watch. An hour to clean up and twenty minutes to shower before she headed to the scavenger hunt starting point to help Kady hand out lists to the participants. She rounded the corner of the empty lounge and came to a dead stop.

Lights had been taken down and placed neatly in their boxes. Banners were folded and stacked on a table. Centerpieces had been tucked into the packing crate marked "centerpieces" in her own loopy handwriting. Someone had obviously gotten up even earlier than she had to clean up on her behalf. Before she registered the obvious answer, a folded note caught her eye. Upon closer inspection, she saw it had her name written on the front. Ignoring the accelerated pounding of her heart, she opened it.

If I were the kind of man who apologized for something he said, this may or may not be how I would go about doing it. Reed.

Julie reread the note five times before she realized her mouth had stretched into a goofy smile.

Chapter Ten

Julie checked her watch, smiling to herself when she saw that the scavenger hunt was set to begin right on schedule. No matter that her friends' postures suggested the only object they were interested in hunting down was a cold, stiff drink. Kady stood beside her holding the stack of lists, preparing to pass them out to the amassing group of wedding guests. Julie had insisted that Kady compile the items to be hunted so she herself could compete. And *win*, if she had her way. More than happy to sip a latte and await the winner in Starbucks, Kady had readily agreed.

Christine stood beside Kady, fussing with her hair. Putting it up in a ponytail, then cursing and letting it back down. She looked hot under the collar about something, but Julie knew better than to ask. They'd often joked that the term "fiery redhead" had been coined on Christine's behalf. Once she got started, they had a hard time calming her back down. Best to let that sleeping dog lie a spell, she decided.

All three of them raised a questioning eyebrow when Regan strolled up and joined them. Wearing a short dress that left little to the imagination and six-inch heels.

"You steal those shoes off a stripper?" Julie asked. "Or are you planning on taking the drastic step of breaking your neck to avoid this scavenger hunt?"

"Actually I'm hoping to distract the competition." Regan posed. "Jealous?"

"Concerned," Kady corrected. "About your ankles. And your mental health."

Regan shrugged, already looking bored.

"Does everyone really want to avoid the scavenger hunt? I thought it would be fun." She felt the familiar stab of disappointment in herself when everyone stayed silent. *Don't let it show.* "Well, that's just dandy."

Reed sauntered up then, standing off to the side of the growing group, arms crossed over his chest. Against her will, every inch of Julie's skin went hypersensitive. Lord, he looked ready for sin. An observation she resented. She didn't want to observe him. Yet she couldn't stop herself from cataloging every part of him. Cut biceps, adorned with tattoos, stretched the sleeves of his white T-shirt in a way that didn't belong among the khaki and polo-shirt-wearing wedding guests. His dark hair was still damp from a shower. She knew from experience now that he would smell fresh, masculine, raw. That underneath that T-shirt and jeans, his body was poised, ready to be exerted. *Craving* exertion. Such a contrast to his deceptively casual pose. When their gazes met, rebellious heat curled below her waist.

No. She didn't want this. Perhaps he'd partially redeemed himself by cleaning up after the party. Easing her burden.

Leaving her that unintentionally sweet, uniquely Reed note. That didn't mean she should excuse last night's lewd comment so easily. Did it? Why did she want to?

Watching Reed, she held out a hand to Kady. "Hand me one of those lists, darlin'."

Regan did a little dance move. "Aw, shit. Julie P on the prowl."

Christine looked amused. Not to mention grateful for a distraction from whatever was obviously giving her fits. "Go easy on him. No one outmatches you when you're holding a list of meaningless items."

"Y'all are seeing things. I just need to clear something up, is all." Julie ignored the round of snorts delivered by her friends and swayed toward Reed, trying for all the world to hide her nerves. At her unexpected approach, he narrowed his eyes, but otherwise didn't move an inch. She lowered her voice so her friends wouldn't overhear their conversation. "If you're expecting a thank-you for acting as my cleanup crew, keep waiting. It won't come. But in the spirit of goodwill I've decided to call us even."

"Is that right, pixie?" He swept her head-to-toe with a blistering look. "I feel obliged to tell you goodwill is the furthest thing from my mind right now."

Julie struggled for composure. She should turn up her nose and walk away. It's what she'd been taught to do when a man overstepped his bounds. They'd gone way past that point, however. She couldn't walk away just then for the life of her. "I've got a scavenger hunt to win. What's on your mind is none of my concern."

"Maybe. But you're hoping I tell you anyway." His attention dropped to her breasts. Julie's face heated, somehow positive he was remembering what they'd done last night at the spring. It made her remember, too. His hands, his mouth. Things he'd said. "I'm thinking about how none of your friends over there know what I found out last night. That you're a kinky little bad girl who likes to be creative. No one here knows. And I fucking love that I do."

Awareness flooded Julie. As if her senses remembered what he could do for her body. The feelings he could elicit with a simple touch or a whispered dare in her ear. She forced herself to remember the crowd of people witnessing their exchange, including her friends, who didn't often see her lose her cool. Friends who would notice immediately if she did. "Enjoy having your secret. Can I trust you to keep it?"

Reed's eyebrows drew together, his voice dropped even lower. "Do you honestly think I would tell one single person? That the blond beauty queen goes off like a firecracker when you stroke her just right? Not a fucking chance, baby. I wouldn't risk someone else trying to take what's—"

"Stop it." Julie's face flamed hot. Her attempts to calm her pounding pulse failed. She couldn't believe the words coming out of his mouth, even though she knew if they were in the dark, she wouldn't be able to get enough. They weren't in the dark, however. And if she listened to him a minute longer, she would combust in front of everyone. Everyone who thought of her as the respectable do-gooder. The planner. The maker-of-pretty. It certainly wouldn't be pretty when she burst into flames. "You've made your point."

"Haven't even begun."

"I say you have."

"Your legs look goddamn incredible in that skirt."

Her rejoinder died in her throat and came out sounding like, "Guhhhh wham."

An uncharacteristic smile shaped his mouth. "Ah, you gotta love a bilingual girl."

"Oh, no. You don't get to be funny, too."

"Too?"

"Here you go." She shoved the scavenger hunt list into his waiting hand and tried to hide her embarrassment with a saucy look. "Think you can keep up?"

"We both know I can keep it up."

Julie spun on a heel and rejoined her friends, sure her face had turned the color of the devil. Sophie had joined the group since Julie left and now observed the building group of wedding guests with apprehension. Absentmindedly, Julie put a calming hand on her shoulder. "Wh-what did I miss?"

They all exchanged a look. "Uh, nothing, Twitchy-Eye. We were watching you have visual intercourse with Mr. Dark and Dangerous," Regan responded drily.

"Hush up. You saw no such thing."

"No, she's right." They all turned to Sophie. "I've only been here a couple minutes, but it was long enough to recognize first class eye-fuckery."

Julie started, her friends breaking into unladylike laughter around her. "Sophie, I don't want to speak too soon, but I think you're starting to come out of your shell."

Sophie shrugged. "So...you and Reed?"

Christine tucked a stray red hair into her ponytail. "I thought you were gunning for the best man."

"Logan," Sophie clarified. "Yeah, what about that?"

"I'd love to indulge all your curiosities, but I believe we're running late—"

"So you're *not* going for Logan?" Regan asked. "Nice. Best man's back on the market." She flexed her fingers and winked. "Game on."

Kady sighed dramatically. "If you ladies are finished proving what a pack of shameless hussies you are, I'd like to pass these lists out and go sit in the air-conditioned coffee shop." She winked at the group. "Colton's been keeping me up late."

"Oh, who's the shameless hussy now?"

Kady laughed, so obviously in love everyone seemed compelled to join in. "Christine, would you mind pairing up with Tyler? I know you've had your differences, but I'm hoping you can take this opportunity to mend fences, so to speak? I just want everyone getting along at my wedding."

Christine clearly wanted to object, but wisely didn't question the bride. She nodded once. "Of course. No problem. Besides, we're *fine*."

Kady shot her a skeptical look, but kept silent.

"Ooh, Kady. Do me a solid and pair me up with Logan." Regan waggled her eyebrows at Julie, who shook her head in response. "If you hear the forest rocking, don't come a-knocking."

"Sorry, he's running late. I'm sending you out with Brock." Kady eyed Regan's shoes. "Anyway, Logan manufactures hiking gear for a living. If he saw you attempting to traverse the woods in stilettos, he'd probably have a coronary." She smiled at Sophie and held out two lists. "Would you wait for Logan, Soph? I don't want him to get here and have no idea what's going on."

"I...uh—" Sophie blushed beet red and started to reply, but Kady simply handed her the lists and moved on to her next target.

"Julie—"

"Oh no," Julie cut her off. "I don't need any deadweight holding me up. No partner for me."

She plucked a list from Kady's hands and sailed off before anyone could protest. No way was she giving her meddling friends the chance to pair her up with Reed. And they would. No question.

But as she entered the forest to retrieve the first item, she could feel brooding hazel eyes following her every step.

• • •

A fucking feather. The second-to-last item on Reed's list. He hadn't even planned on participating in this ridiculous scavenger hunt, the prize for which happened to be some souped-up, bells-and-whistles coffee machine he wouldn't be caught dead using. An hour later, he was ready to climb a tree and pluck a feather out of a damn woodpecker just to bring him one step closer to finishing. If Julie hadn't handed him the list with a blatant challenge in her eyes, he would have tossed it in the nearest trash can and gone for a beer. Instead, he'd chosen to see the subtle tilt of her head and pursing of her pink lips as a thrown-down gauntlet. He'd had no choice but to take it.

Reed nudged aside a pile of pine needles with his boot, finding nothing but more pine needles. Edging around the tree, he found a feather stuck in the bark, but came up short when he saw a flash of pink enter his line of vision. Julie. Shoving the feather in his pocket absentmindedly, he watched with rapt attention as she bent over, revealing those long legs to perfection in her lightweight skirt. When she straightened again, she held a pinecone in her hand as if it were a winning lottery ticket, before shoving it into her tote bag.

"What exactly does a scavenger hunt have to do with two people getting married?"

She jerked around at the sound of his voice.

"Unless, of course, we're searching for their lost minds."

Blue eyes narrowed on him. "You know what you are? A sourpuss." She started to bypass him on the trail, grumbling to herself. "Out here ruining everyone's good time. Wouldn't know fun if it bit him on his keister."

In a replay of the night before, he strode after her. "Maybe our idea of fun is just different. That doesn't mean I don't know how to have it."

"Oh, I know your idea of fun."

"Hell, we hadn't even gotten to the good part yet."

She pulled her tote bag higher on her shoulder and increased her pace, tennis shoes kicking up dust in her effort to leave him behind. "I don't expect we will, either."

"That so?"

"Mmm-hmm. If I were a Magic 8 Ball, my answer would read 'outlook not so good.'"

"Why don't you let me shake you up a little? See if we can't get a different answer."

"My sources say no."

Reed swallowed a laugh. Damn it, she was a feisty little thing. An image flashed through his mind of Julie astride him, hips undulating, head thrown back in ecstasy, and he groaned out loud. She sent him a wary look over her shoulder but didn't stop. If he didn't find a way to appeal to her, the vision would never become a reality. "I guess you don't want to hear the challenge, then."

Julie came to a halt and he nearly crashed into her back. "What now?"

He hid his smile. Underneath all that charm, he knew he'd sensed a competitor. Based on the contents of her bag, she'd nearly finished the damn hunt. Sure, his list was almost completed, too, but then he was a trained law officer. "How many items do you have left on your list?"

"One."

"Same here."

Her confidence slipped a little. "So?"

Reed shrugged. "Just thought you might care to make it interesting."

"Next you're going to taunt me. Say something like, 'But if you're not confident in your abilities, I understand.'"

"You said it, not me."

She whispered something under her breath that sounded like *hellfire*, but he couldn't be sure. Shifting on her feet, she considered him. "What are your terms, sourpuss?"

"Ladies first."

Her arms crossed over her chest, enjoyment finally entering her eyes, and Reed barely resisted the urge to breathe a sigh of relief. "If I find my item first, you show up to dance rehearsals tomorrow evening in a tuxedo. Not one word of complaint while Francois teaches everyone the waltz."

He winced a little. Couldn't help it. "That's his name? Francois?" When she merely raised an eyebrow, he sighed. "Deal."

"What are your terms?"

Reed knew Julie wouldn't like his idea, so he took a step closer in case she tried to storm off. To his surprise, she didn't back down when he brought their bodies flush, ran a hand over her hip, and let it linger there. "I assume, as part of these pole dancing classes, you learn how to...dance? Without the pole, I mean."

"I know what you mean," Julie replied hastily, a flush moving up her neck. He wanted to follow it with his mouth. "There might be...*some* of that involved," she said shakily.

"Good." His hand slipped across her shoulder to massage the back of her neck in slow circles with his thumb. "If I win, you dance for me. In my room. All of your clothes come off."

She swallowed audibly. "Won't that lead to sex?"

"Only if you want it to." He brushed his lips over hers. "You don't have to second-guess what I want. I'd take you right here if you asked me to."

A whimper slipped past her lips. "I agree to your terms." When her hands went to his belt buckle, Reed's stomach muscles clenched. Their gazes connected. "That said, I wouldn't mind getting a little preview."

Reed pushed himself into her hands. "Take me out, then, baby. I'm already hard from watching you prance around in that little pink skirt."

She lowered his fly and pushed his jeans down over his hips. Her words whispered across his mouth. "You want to give it to me hard, Reed?"

"You've never had it as hard as I'm going to give it to you." Brain sufficiently scrambled, he captured her mouth in a slippery kiss, nipping her bottom lip as he pulled back. "What changed your mind? The cleaning?"

Julie hooked her thumbs into his boxers and slipped them down his legs, then rose to trace the skin under his jaw with her damp, parted lips. "I love a man who cleans." She pulled back a little, teased his mouth with a swift kiss. "But I was the Tri Delt scavenger hunt champion four years in a row. I never, ever lose."

Before Reed could ascertain her intention, Julie took off running for the resort, leaving him there in the woods with his pants and boxer shorts tangled around his ankles. With a hard-on to beat the band. Torn between fury, unbelievable pain, and grudging admiration, he yanked his pants up and took off after her. "I'm going to make you pay for that one, pixie."

"It was worth it," she yelled back over her shoulder, at least one hundred yards ahead of him on the trail. The resort became visible in the distance and he picked up his pace. So did Julie. Her feet were a blur as she sprinted along the concrete. It became apparent to Reed in that moment that he'd seriously underestimated the pixie.

"What's your last item on the list?"

"A bell." She didn't even have the decency to sound winded. "You?"

"A newspaper." He laughed. "Face it baby, I've got you beat. No way do you find a bell first."

"Oh, yeah? Watch me."

"Get ready to dance."

"A victory dance, you mean?" Julie glanced back at him, humor lighting her face. Then, as if she hadn't surprised him enough today, she mocked him, throwing his own words back in his face. "What changed your mind, baby? The cleaning?"

"Oh, you are asking for it now." Suddenly, she veered to

the left and took the path leading toward the hotel lobby. He followed right behind her as she threw open the heavy wooden door and entered the lobby at a dead run. Customers watched curiously as they raced past the plush seating area, dodging luggage carts and stray suitcases as they headed for the check-in area. An older man stepped into Reed's path, forcing him to slow as Julie reached the front desk first.

When he realized her plan, his booming laugh echoed across the lobby.

Chapter Eleven

Julie heaved the entire stack of newspapers onto the front desk and smiled at the dumbfounded attendant. "I'd like to buy all of them, please."

The young man studied her for a second, as if looking for signs of mental illness, then shrugged. Julie felt Reed come up behind her just as he finished counting the newspapers. She pulled a twenty-dollar bill from her skirt pocket and laid it on the counter, giving the young man her best smile as she did so. To her left, Reed sighed loudly. She ignored him.

"You wouldn't happen to have any more in the back, would you, sugar? I'm in a bit of a pinch, you see. I've organized a papier-mâché craft hour for the children attending the wedding. Would you believe I went and forgot to bring newspaper? The main ingredient. Sometimes I think I'd forget my feet if I didn't need them to walk. How long have you been working here? If I had to hazard a guess, I'd say quite a while. You've got an air of confidence about you.

Yes sir, you do. My Aunt Sylvie always said that a confident man writes his own ticket in this world. Would you mind checking on those newspapers, darlin'? Bless your heart."

As the young man turned, looking more than a little thunderstruck, toward the back office, Reed leaned over and spoke quietly in her ear. She tried unsuccessfully to ignore the hot shiver that ran down her spine. Try as she might, nothing could stop him from affecting her. She'd wanted him on the mountain to a stunning degree, had barely managed to hold back. "You can try to prevent me from getting a newspaper, but what about your bell? You still need one to—"

Without batting an eyelash, Julie slipped the front desk bell into her tote bag. Ignoring Reed's look of shocked reproach, she tucked a stack of newspapers under each arm and took off in the direction of Starbucks, where Kady was waiting to crown the winner. She glanced back to find Reed breaking into a jog after her and she couldn't help but laugh. The look on his face suggested he hated losing just as much as she did. Deciding the newspapers were weighing her down, she set them on a high table and made a break for it. Even if he picked up one of the papers and tried to catch her, Starbucks was so close that he'd never catch—

The optimistic thought died in its inception when two strong arms snagged her around the middle, catching her in mid-stride. Even if she hadn't caught his oaky sent, the wide chest she was pulled back against would have told her it was Reed. Before Julie could protest, he pulled her from the lobby into an adjacent hallway, which led to a series of first-floor rooms. As the sounds of people and rolling luggage faded away, their labored breathing was the only sound that remained. He let her drop to her feet and pushed her against the wall. Suddenly, Julie felt basely desperate for him. Her body begged for his. Adrenaline, the remnants of their fight, the challenge he'd given her on the hunt, had heightened her already-colossal attraction to him. Yet even knowing that, she wanted him with a fierceness that made her moan and close her eyes when he fit their bodies together.

One calloused hand slid up the back of her bare thigh, disappearing beneath her skirt. When it reached her bottom, he palmed it roughly once, then boosted her higher to fit his erection between her legs. Julie's head fell back against the wall on a gasp. "Any other day, I'd let you get away with that little stunt. Not today. Not when winning means a private striptease from the girl who's been keeping my cock permanently hard. A striptease that ends in me fucking her into next week."

Her breath shuddered out. "Y-you didn't win either."

In his left hand, Reed held up a single newspaper, then let it drop. "We'll keep it between us."

His hips flexed and Julie bit her lip hard. She could feel the flesh between her legs clench reflexively and go damp at the thought of Reed inside her. Nothing mattered at that moment, apart from the need. Not their differences or what would come afterward. Julie couldn't see past playing out her hottest fantasy. Dancing for this man. Tempting him. Finally being seen as something other than efficient and pretty to look at. She'd never wanted anything quite so badly.

"Take me to your room."

Reed kissed her once, long and hard, growling in his throat the whole time. Tangling her fingers in his hair, wanting to get lost in the kiss, she protested when he abruptly backed away, but he simply grabbed her hand and led her down the corridor, turning right at the end and stopping at the second door. Once inside, she expected him to kiss her, throw her on the bed, and finally slake the incessant hunger. Instead, he unbuttoned his shirt slowly, watching her closely like a predator, eyes heavy with arousal. In other words, no way was he letting her forget about their agreement or allowing them to become distracted. Good. Julie didn't want to forget about it, but now that the moment had arrived, she didn't know where to start. She worked in the liquor business. In the South, no less. A man's world that she'd had to bust her behind to infiltrate. And despite what Reed thought, organizing a destination wedding was no walk in the park, either. This was just a simple dance. One she'd walked into with her eyes wide open.

Now or never, Julie.

Doing her best to look confident, she grabbed an armless desk chair, pulling it to the base of the bed. With a toss of her hair, she indicated for him to sit. Now shirtless, he dropped into the chair and stretched out his long legs in front of him without breaking eye contact. Hair tousled from pulling his undershirt over his head, tattoos and scars spreading across his muscled chest and abdomen, he looked criminally sexy, but the rapid pulse at his neck gave him away. He was just as affected as she was. That telltale sign shot her full of confidence, making her feel hot, desirable.

"Are you sure you want this?" Julie asked him. She pressed a button on the clock radio, stopping when she landed on a station playing what sounded like tribal music. At once, her pulse beat faster in time with the drums. Excitement swirled in her belly. "Once I start, I'm not going to stop until you can't take anymore."

Reed's mouth parted in surprise, but he hid the reaction quickly. "I can more than handle a lap dance, baby. What I can't handle is waiting. Get started."

Julie's lips spread into a slow smile as she sauntered forward, stopping between his outstretched legs. Supporting herself on his shoulders, she bent forward slowly to speak right next to his ear. "No touching."

"I know the rules."

"Maybe. Doesn't mean you won't try to break them."

"Why are your clothes still on?"

She bit his earlobe and tugged. "So impatient."

Reed hissed a breath. "If you only knew the things I want to do to you, pixie, you'd already be underneath me with your legs in the air, screaming loud enough to shatter glass."

"All in good time," she countered, straightening once more. One deep breath for courage and she started to move. She released her hair from its ponytail and shook it out, combing her fingers through it slowly in a way she knew made her breasts strain against her tank top. Anticipation laced with excitement made her nipples pebble. She watched Reed's chest rise and fall faster as he noticed. Wanting to keep his eyes there, she ran her hands down slowly over the swells of her breasts, giving them a light squeeze that had him shifting in the chair.

"Let me see them. Let me see where I've been."

Ducking her head and looking at him through her eyelashes, she let her hips begin to sway, drawing his attention away from her chest. Her hands smoothed down over her thighs, lingering at the vee between her legs, before sliding back up to the hem of her shirt. Inch by inch, she lifted it, revealing her naked breasts. She tossed the garment at Reed. He caught it in midair and threw it across the room without looking away from her once.

"Jesus. I only got to see them in the dark last night... your breasts were made for sucking on, Julie." He leaned back in the chair, stroked his fly with the heel of his hand. "When I used my mouth on you, I could taste how much you wanted to have me between those breasts. Tasted sweet as fuck."

His words startling a moan from her throat, Julie's hands rose of their own accord to circle her thumbs around her nipples. She continued the smooth figure-eight motions of her hips, the combined movements causing fire to lick over her skin. Seeing Reed looking so incredibly turned on triggered answering sensations throughout her body. Flames that she needed him to extinguish. Just not *yet*. Not until the entire fantasy played out. Not until she drove him past his breaking point.

Placing her hands on his shoulders, she danced just close enough that the tips of her breasts swayed in front of his parted mouth with her every sensual movement. Reed's guttural groan bathed her nipples in heat. Heat that shot straight to her core, making her muscles contract and release. Making her damp and achy. Reed's hands rose as if to fondle her breasts, but she shook her head in reproach and moved away slightly as punishment.

"Know what I think, baby? You love making my cock hard. You've been living for it since that first night." He leaned forward slightly, gaze riveted on her chest. "I've been living for it, too. I've been stroking myself off to the memory of how you looked at me on that patio. Like you were a little nervous and a lot turned on. Did you go back to your seat in the fancy restaurant and cross your legs tighter than before? Were you planning on going back to your room later that night and imagining the big bad man touching your pussy?"

"*Yes.*"

Yearning, dizzyingly potent, rocketed through Julie, so swift she feared her knees might buckle. She turned slowly, so he couldn't see how much his uncensored speech affected her. Increasing the pace of her hips, she hooked her thumbs into the waistband of her skirt and tugged it down just enough that he could see the top of her silky teal-colored thong. The performance, her secret fantasy come to life, emboldened her. Made her want to shock him back. She flicked her hair over her shoulder and looked at him through hooded eyes. "If I had pleasured myself that night, Reed, you wouldn't have been touching me with your hand. In my fantasy, you would have been deep, deep inside of me. Telling me what a bad thing I'd done."

"What bad thing did you do, baby?" His voice sounded raw.

"When you showed up at the party, I might have gone to the bathroom and…hiked my skirt up a little higher for you. I knew you'd be watching me."

"Sweet fucking hell."

Julie let her skirt drop, leaving her in nothing but the minuscule panties. Reed's loud groan caused any lingering self-consciousness to fade as Julie arched her back, bent her knees and ground her hips as low as she could go toward the ground. He let out a string of curses as she rose gradually, dancing erotically to the pounding beat of the music.

"Come closer, baby. Need you closer. *Now*, pixie."

The desire in his voice tore at her own, sending it clamoring through her system. She needed to be closer, to touch, just as badly as he needed it. Still facing away from him, she gripped his knees and lowered her bottom onto his lap, gasping at the hardness she encountered. She switched her hips from a circular motion to a gentle front-to-back tease that allowed her to ride his length base to tip. "You like that, sugar?" she whispered, barely audible among the bass-heavy music.

He released a strangled growl against her neck. "Enough teasing. Sit down all the way and work my cock with your beautiful ass. No more games."

Julie closed her eyes and released a shaky breath. This had started as *her* seduction, but she was quickly being driven crazy by the man beneath her. Reed might not be touching her with his hands, but his body radiated heat, promise, need. In electrifying waves. And Julie was quickly going under.

"Like this?" She leaned back on his chest and draped her legs over his strong thighs. Dropping her head back onto his shoulder, she gave him a view down her body as she undulated on his lap, his erection wedged snugly against her bottom, pulsing, lengthening. Ever so slightly, his hips pumped in a rolling, upward motion, stealing her sanity.

"Call me sugar again."

"Like this, sugar?"

"Yes, sexy girl. Just like that." He bit into her shoulder, thrusting up hard at the same time. "Feel that? Feel what you did?"

"Yes." She moaned. "I feel it."

"You want it?"

She nodded frantically.

"I'm warning you right now, it's going to be a rough ride. If you're not ready for it yet, I'll put you on your knees for a while to take my edge off."

Julie's heart pounded so loud, it felt like it might exit her chest. His words were pushing her past her breaking point. Words that should offend her, alarm her. Instead, she only wanted *more*. She wanted Reed's brand of rough. Wanted to be the object of his lust, his reason for losing control.

When she slipped a hand underneath the waistband of her panties, his breathing grew even more labored. She found the bundle of nerves, aching for his touch, and circled her middle finger around it once. "I don't want your edge off. I don't want to be treated like a lady." She tipped her head to the side, whimpering as his lips licked and sucked at her neck. "I want you to deliver on all the promises you've made. I want everything you've got."

At once, he surged out of the chair with a growl, carrying her with him. He pushed her down over a smooth cedar bureau, bent over with her hips in the air, and yanked the panties down her legs. Julie looked at her reflection in the attached mirror, amazed at the woman staring back at her. She looked drugged, desperate, out of control. Such a departure from her usual unruffled composure. Behind her, Reed's features were drawn together tightly as he ripped open a condom wrapper and rolled it down his thick length with jerky movements.

With one powerful drive, Reed finally entered her. The pressure was so great, so delicious, that Julie bit her lip and screamed, hands scrambling for purchase on the wood bureau top. Through partially blind eyes, she looked up at Reed's reflection to find an expression of undiluted pleasure on his face. But it quickly transformed into a need for more, as he wrapped her hair around his fist and jerked it back.

"You will never dance like that again. You will *never* hike your skirt up again. Never." He pulled out slightly, then thrust back into her hard. "Not unless it's for me. Is that understood?"

Julie cried out. "*Yes*."

"Not good enough." He hooked his arm under her left knee and yanked it waist-level, grunting in satisfaction as his hips pumped, driving deeper with each upward push. The position made her arch her back in a way that put him right where she needed him, every thrust finding its mark. "Say, 'Yes, Reed, I understand. I'll be a good girl from now on.'"

When she didn't answer fast enough, he bit her shoulder in warning. "I'll be a good girl," she half sobbed, half whispered.

He dropped his head forward on a groan and increased his pace, pinning Julie's hips to the hard surface, forcing her to receive his rigid arousal over and over, until her legs began to quake, her skin started to prickle with the oncoming orgasm.

"You're starting to tighten up on me, baby. Do you want my fingers to massage you between your legs?"

"God, yes. *Please*."

"No."

Their gazes connected in the mirror. Hers frantic, questioning. His, unreadable. "That first night, I told you, no touching yourself. Not even with your right hand. You broke the rule during your little dance. You can't have my fingers."

"*Reed*."

His dark laughter grazed her neck. "I'll make an exception. If you accept a different punishment later, I'll rub your hot little clit right now."

"Fine…just…oh, please."

"Is that a yes?"

"Yes!"

The arm beneath her knee tightened and yanked her leg even higher, propping it on the bureau. Leaving her provocatively exposed in a way that stole oxygen from her lungs. His thrusts became longer, more measured as he reached around to slide two fingers on either side of her clitoris. He pinched it lightly between his knuckles and squeezed, before giving her what she needed. The pads of his middle and ring finger petted her delicately at first, then faster and with more pressure. Julie could only shut her eyes and accept the tumult of sensations as they began lashing mercilessly at her body. His erection moved, thick and unyielding, inside of her, Reed pounding out his own need while lengthening her powerful climax. Shattering every notion she'd ever had about intimacy.

She felt him pulse hot inside of her, stretching her, ready to give in. He gripped her chin and lifted her head so it faced the mirror. "Watch me. Watch me finish, baby. You need to see what you did." When she nodded, his movements grew jerky, yet somehow even more determined. Ever so slightly, he tightened his grip on her jaw until her mouth opened from the pressure. He pushed his fingers inside. "Suck."

Julie didn't question, she simply closed her lips around his fingers, drew on them as hard as she could. And watched Reed come apart behind her.

Chapter Twelve

Reed cinched the white towel around his waist and stared blindly at his reflection in the fogged-up bathroom mirror. For the first time since he could remember, he wondered what someone else thought when they looked at him. Ugly, painful-looking scars, one at his hip, another slashing down from his collarbone. An unruly mess of tattoos running together, none of them with any particular meaning except to cover him up. To keep people away.

Why hadn't it worked with Julie?

Not wanting to look at himself any longer, he turned and leaned back on the marble sink, crossing his arms over his chest. And tried not to blink. Every time he closed his eyes, he saw her in the mirror. Hair a gorgeous mess, lips swollen and damp, breasts bouncing up and down from the force of his thrusts.

"Hell." Reed dragged his hands down his face, feeling himself harden beneath the towel. Thank Christ she'd gone back to her room to shower, or they'd be at it again. Not that it had been easy letting her walk out of the room, looking more than a little shell-shocked by their heated encounter, followed by his sudden silence. His less-than-warm treatment of her after the hottest damn sex of his life. He'd wanted to say something to make her smile, but the words never came.

Truthfully, he still couldn't come up with words to describe what the hell had taken place between them. Consensual sex between two adults didn't cover it. He'd demanded *promises* from her; he'd held nothing of himself back. Two things he'd never done, not with any woman. When he'd tried to chalk it up to the heat of the moment, he immediately discarded the notion. An hour later, the thought of another man looking at her, watching her dance, made him grind his knuckles into the counter. He couldn't even contemplate it without adrenaline blasting through his veins, demanding more assurances from her.

Where the hell did he get off asking for reassurance? Promises? He had no use for them. Certainly couldn't make any of his own. He'd break them...wouldn't he? Broken promises were his legacy. They ran in his family. Julie probably came from a long line of honorable men who kept their word. Men whose word meant something in the first place.

She'd marry a man like that someday.

Long minutes passed before Reed could think clearly again, the idea of Julie marrying another man having wrapped around his throat to choke him. He sucked in a deep breath and left the bathroom to go dress. What were his options? Option one: cut things off with Julie now, try to keep his distance from her the rest of the week, and never see her again? Reed almost laughed. He'd nearly gone to her seconds after she left his room this afternoon. Four more days? Not a hope in hell of his lasting that long. They hadn't even spoken about the fact that they lived in the same city. If he didn't get rid of this infatuation *now*, knowing she was so close would drive him slowly insane.

That left him with option two: stop thinking so damn much, make the most of the time she allowed him, and fuck her so well, so thoroughly, she would never forget him for the rest of her perfect, privileged life.

Option two it is.

Reed yanked a black T-shirt over his head and strode to the door. He paused with his hand on the knob. Perhaps this decision wasn't exactly wise. The pull he felt toward Julie wouldn't lessen the more time he spent with her. It might even strengthen. Reed rested his forehead against the door. He thought of her alone in her room, wondering if she'd done something wrong. Wondering if she'd ever feel him inside her again. It made him crazy. He didn't know where this urge to soothe, to reassure, came from. It felt primitive. As if it had always been there, sitting unused in some hidden part of him, gaining strength. Now the urge blasted him like volcanic ash. She would be *his* Julie. At least for the next four days.

The second he referred to Julie as *his*, the jealous beast within him lay down, relaxed for the first time since she'd left. He didn't know what that meant, only that if he stayed away from her, the anxious feeling would return. Decision made, he left the room at a brisk pace.

Minutes later, he stood outside her door, impatient to see her. Before he could knock, he heard her muffled voice on the other side, sounding upset. Only *her* voice, however, suggesting she was alone. On the phone, possibly? Reed glanced down the hallway, knowing he should leave. Let her deal with her problem and return later, pretending he'd never heard the tinge of sadness in her voice.

Instead, he found himself knocking. When she pulled the door open, cell phone pressed to her ear, Reed felt something odd, something foreign move in his chest. Inside a puffy white robe that fairly swallowed her, bare feet poking out at the bottom, she looked so incredibly sweet and defenseless, he could only stare at her. Then he heard the angry voice on the other end of the phone and his body went on alert. He noticed her deflated posture for the first time, the downturned corners of her mouth. Someone was upsetting Julie and that definitely didn't work for him.

Reed opened his mouth to demand the phone from her, but managed to hold himself back at the last second. *Shit. Shit, I really need to get a handle on this. I'm acting like a lunatic.*

"You're right, Daddy, I picked an inconvenient time to leave Atlanta." Julie dropped her hand from the door, but left it open as she retreated into the room. Reed stepped in and closed the door behind him without taking his eyes off her. She sank down onto the edge of the bed and massaged her forehead. "Have you tried calling Dr. Cybil? She makes house calls." She listened for a moment. "Good…I just…I didn't expect this. Last year, when we reached three years, Mom seemed to be coping better. I would never have left if I'd—"

She broke off as Reed sat down next to her on the bed. He hadn't planned on it, had been walking toward the balcony to get some air and wait for her to wrap up the call. Then her words had started making sense, calling to mind the conversation he'd overhead between Julie and her mother. Three years. Her sister's death. Hell, he'd been so wrapped up in his own bullshit, his almost-painful attraction to her, he'd let it slip from his mind. She'd opened up to him in the woods and he'd basically disregarded it. Just another way they differed. If Julie knew someone was hurting, she would probably do everything to fix it. He, on the other hand, just expected everyone to bottle it up and move on. Like he did. Funny, he didn't want Julie to bottle anything up. Not around him. Even as the idea of shouldering someone else's burdens terrified him, he craved the idea of bearing the brunt of anything upsetting Julie.

With considerable effort, Reed pushed aside the startling realization. Trying for casual, he laid his hand on top of hers, all the while pretending to be engrossed in the muted television. Her hand jerked a little and for a brief, awful moment, he thought she might pull away. After casting him a quick glance, she slowly entwined her fingers with his and continued her conversation, voice a hint more confident than before. Why that made him so goddamn happy, he didn't have the courage to explore.

"Daddy, we know the cycle by now. She won't stay in bed forever…just give her time." Julie cleared her throat, shifting on the bed. "Does she…does she want to talk to me?" She nodded once. "Okay, then. Call me back if she changes her mind."

Reed watched her hand drop into her lap, the phone call ended. He waited for her to say something, because hell, Julie *always* had something to say. Frankly, he was counting on it, because he didn't know the first thing about comforting a woman. He racked his brain for inspiration. None came. So he simply went with his gut. "What was she like?" He swallowed hard. "Serena, I mean."

Julie was silent a moment. "Quiet. Compassionate. Loving." She exhaled. "People would mistake it for weakness sometimes but we all knew better. She could cut you off at the knees with a smile on her face." She reached up and released her hair from the haphazard bun on her head. "Serena loved the rain. I never understood that about her. She sat with me for hours, watching it through the window. We used to play go fish, waiting for it to let up. She was so patient and all I ever did was complain about wanting to go outside. Now...I love the rain. I was too young to understand her then, and now that I do, it's too late." A long pause. "She was better than me, Reed. Sometimes, I think it should have been—"

"Stop. Don't say it." Reed's hand tightened reflexively on hers. "Promise me you won't ever say that out loud." He glanced away, more than a little unnerved by his reaction. "I didn't know her, but she wasn't better than you. Different doesn't mean better." He looked back to find those big blue eyes trained on him. "I'm still waiting on that promise."

"I promise."

Reed nodded once. "Good." She merely watched him silently, and he cursed. "I don't get it, pixie. With everyone else, you talk a mile a minute. But you get around me and you go quiet. For once, I wouldn't mind it if you ran your mouth for a while."

She laughed. Not a regular laugh, but that loud, cracking laugh that he'd only heard once before. The one that made his throat feel uncomfortably tight. When it died down, she shook her head. "What are you doing here, Reed?"

"You know why I'm here."

With a sigh, Julie stood up and walked through the balcony doors. Reed followed, joining her where she leaned against the wooden rail. Late afternoon had fallen over the mountains in the distance, casting shadows and light patterns over the vast resort. A light breeze lifted the blond hair off Julie's shoulder. Reed shook himself, wondering when the hell he'd started noticing such details. "I suppose I do."

"You suppose nothing." He took a step closer, pressed his mouth to the skin beneath her ear. "I'm already hard and aching again, baby. Shouldn't have let you leave my room."

"Let me?" She tipped her head to the side and exposed her neck for his mouth, teeth sinking into the plump flesh of her bottom lip when he grazed her with his stubbled chin. "You couldn't get me out the door fast enough."

Reed frowned, pulled back. He opened his mouth to deny it, but the lie wouldn't come. Only the truth. At least as he saw it. "You already know I don't do the romantic afterglow. If that's what you want..." He broke off. If that's what you want—*what?* Let's part ways? Go find someone else? *Fuck, no.* But he didn't know how to finish the damn sentence. Julie watched him, patiently waiting. He swallowed heavily and went to sit on the white wicker chair near the wall. "What can I say? I'm an emotionless son of a bitch. It's why I'm good at what I do. Everything is black and white. No gray areas to get lost in."

Surprise written on her features, she lowered herself into the chair opposite him. She seemed to be choosing her words. "I have to say, I envy that. Working with family...it's a lot of softening your opinion to save people's feelings. Half the time, you end up offending them anyway. Your job might be more dangerous, but at least it's all about bagging and tagging the bad guy. No questions asked."

A laugh escaped him, sounding odd to his ears. "Bagging and tagging? Pretty ruthless, pixie. Maybe you're in the wrong line of work."

Amusement playing around her mouth, she shrugged daintily. "I think I'd make a fine policewoman. Anyone gets unruly and I'll just talk them to death."

"That's my line."

"Thought I'd beat you to it."

Reed rubbed a hand along his chin, trying to get rid of the damn smile. "Nah, you might look hot as hell in the uniform, but you're too soft, baby. You'd want to give everyone the benefit of the doubt. Sometimes it's just not possible."

"I'm not soft. Not always," she murmured.

The change in her tone kicked up his heart rate. "Come over here and prove it."

A flush spread up her neck. "What did you have in mind?"

Reed knew what he was doing. The conversation, the mood between them, had turned too comfortable, too damn perfect, and this was his way of putting them back on a playing field with which he felt familiar. Even knowing his reasons didn't stop him. It only encouraged the change. He didn't know any other way. "Get over here. Don't make me ask again."

For long seconds, she looked thrown off by the change in him. *No*, he decided. She looked excited by it. She wet her lips, palms running the length of her thighs. Finally, she rose and came toward him. When she paused a few feet away, he narrowed his eyes to draw her closer.

"You asked for my fingers earlier in exchange for a punishment later. Time's up, pixie."

With a shuddering exhale, she stepped in between his legs, gasping as he reached up to undo the tie of her robe. "Reed…someone might see…"

"I told you once before I would never allow someone to see you like this." He yanked the tie hard. The robe fell open. "Are you doubting me?"

"No," she whispered.

He parted the sides of her robe, swallowing a groan when he found her naked beneath the fluffy material. Her smooth skin looked flushed, soft and pink from her shower. Simultaneously, he leaned forward and pulled her toward him so he could bury his nose in her belly button, inhaling the peach scent he would forever associate with her. Fingers slipped into his hair hesitantly, holding him there. He wanted to stay there indefinitely, but it felt too good, so he pulled back. "Straddle my thighs."

Julie's body jolted a little at the steel in his voice, but using his shoulders for balance, she did as he asked. Opening herself to him. Naked, save the robe draped on either side of his legs, core exposed by her spread position, she embodied temptation. Reed was forced to unzip his jeans to accommodate his surging erection. Her willingness to trust him, to let him bring her pleasure in ways she was unfamiliar with, wreaked havoc on his mind. His body. He rewarded her by sucking her nipples, flicking and rubbing them with his tongue until her hips began to shift in the air, seeking pressure she wouldn't find. Knowing her sex trembled for satisfaction, but wouldn't get it unless he allowed it to happen, made Reed groan around the beautifully formed nipple in his mouth. Made him draw on it harder. Blindly, he tore a condom from his pocket and rolled it on.

"Reed. Please t-touch me. I need you to touch me."

His hands slid up the backs of her thighs to her ass, gripped the flesh hard. Her breathy whimper shot lust straight to his belly. "Every time you ask, I'll make you wait longer." The hands on his shoulders flexed as she nodded, expression pained. Taking his time, Reed trailed his hands down her legs and around to the juncture of her thighs. "I'm going to spank you, pixie. But not in the way you expect." His grip on her thighs tightened punishingly. "These legs… the objects of my frustration." One hand moved higher to palm her pussy. "I know they lead straight to here. That's what fucks me up, baby. Now it's going to feel the sting."

Then he gently slapped her between the legs. Her gasp of shock turned into a moan as her knees buckled. With a growl, Reed quickly put her back in a standing position. And did it again. And again. The light slapping sounds of his hand connecting with her wet center drove him wild. If he allowed it to continue, he wouldn't last five minutes. Indulging himself, he slapped her delicate heat once more, right over the spot begging for attention. Julie's grip on his shoulders trembled; her legs began to shake. He moved on, slapping the sensitive skin of her inner thighs. The backs, the sides.

"Hiked your skirt up for me, is that right? Did you think you'd get away with that?"

"No." Her chest shuddered. "I don't know."

"You don't *know*?"

Julie leaned down and tried to kiss him, but he jerked back, wanting an explanation. She finally answered on a breath. "I didn't *want* to get away with it."

He groaned his pleasure. "That's what I thought. Mine from the beginning." Jerking the robe off her shoulders, Reed grasped her buttocks and sat her down on his erection, filling her to the hilt. He swooped down with his mouth to swallow her scream, loving the taste of her desperation on his tongue. Already she'd begun to tighten and shudder around him. The driving need for her to move mingled with delicious frustration. "Goddammit." Flexing his hips, he groaned. "I knew that first night. From the way you walked. Moved. I knew you'd be tight as fuck, Julie."

Her mouth opened on his neck, voice barely audible. "That's the first time you've called me by my actual name."

Reed ceased all movement, her words ringing in his ears. He shook his head, dislodging her mouth. "No. No, that can't be right."

Julie kissed his lips, leaning back to meet his eyes when he didn't kiss her back. Before she could question him, he stood and carried her into the room, still planted firmly inside her. With each step, she caught her breath at the way she bounced on his hardness, legs circling his hips, clinging. Reed could barely think over the buzzing in his ears. The realization that he'd never called her by her name made him fucking crazy. It hit too close to home, a painful reminder of his past. He had to make it right, immediately. She deserved more.

Reed laid her down on the bed, pushing deep, *deep*, until she shook underneath him. "Julie," he whispered in her ear. Savoring her moan, he took her knees in his hands and pushed them wide. He wanted to shout at the goddamn perfection of her. Jesus, she'd been formed just for him.

Was such a thing even possible? Then he slid out of her, thrusting back in slowly, forcing himself to take his time. Go slow and let himself savor her. He worked his pelvis in a hot, deliberately slow bump-and-grind, delivering pressure and friction to her sweet spot. "*Julie*." Reed took her hands in his and pinned them over her head, driving into her at an accelerating pace. He couldn't help it with the way she continued to tighten around him. She arched her back and moaned, pink-tipped breasts jutting toward him, begging for a lick. He found an angle with his hips that made her fingernails dig into his restraining hands, felt her start to lose control. As she reached her peak, he drew on her nipples. The sounds of his sucking combined with her throaty cries of his name to push him over the edge.

When he came, he buried his face in her neck and chanted her name. Over and over in her ear.

Chapter Thirteen

Julie woke with a jolt when her cell phone buzzed on the table beside the bed. Realizing in shock that night had long-since fallen and she'd been out of contact for hours, she tried to sit up but couldn't. An arm around her middle kept her pinned to the bed. It seemed the shocks were far from over. Reed lay beside her, illuminated by the muted television, flickering shadows lighting his broad, muscular chest and stubborn face. Even in sleep he looked obstinate, Julie mused, unable to stop her smile. It vanished almost immediately. What did she think she was doing?

Their afternoon-turned-evening together played through her mind in a series of blatantly erotic images. The things he'd done to her. Things she'd wanted him to do. Begged him to do. He'd brought something to life in her. Something that had perhaps always been there, but no one had ever made her want to embrace. Prior to meeting Reed, she would have scoffed at the very idea of being ordered around by a man in the bedroom. She would have thought it made a woman soft. Weak. Yet she'd felt the complete opposite of weak. She'd felt powerful. Desirable. Hadn't wanted it to end.

This man has the ability to turn you inside out.

The harsh thought came unbidden to her mind, smacking of absolute truth. Reed could barely stand to be touched in a nonsexual way, didn't have an affectionate bone in his body. He dominated. Wrung pleasure out of her ruthlessly. But that didn't equate to caring for her. She needed to remember that. They were a temporary fling. They would both go back to Atlanta, to their very different lives, and possibly never cross paths again, being that they ran in such vastly different circles. To his credit, he'd told her he didn't do romance. Not that it had been necessary for him to put into words what was already so obvious. She didn't *want* romance from him, either. Right? Waking up next to him, however, seeing him in the vulnerable state of sleep, feeling his warm body wrapped protectively around hers…it didn't exactly inspire her to keep a rational, level head about his intentions.

Like it or not, what they'd done together required a certain level of trust. Allowing him to dominate her, hold her down, punish her, had created a tenuous bond between them in her mind. A fact that terrified her, because it would inevitably be severed at some point. By him. Her. Their differences. She didn't know. Only that it would happen.

Knowing she needed to get up, attend to her responsibilities, Julie took one last opportunity to look him over. Commit him to memory. After all, who knew how long this would continue? That first night, Regan had described him as tall, dark, and dangerous. The description certainly fit, but much more lurked under his rough, damaged exterior. He harbored pain and insecurities, same as everyone else. Only she suspected his wounds ran much deeper. They'd been inflicted by others he should have been able to trust, giving him ample reason to keep people at a distance. Sure, losing Serena had been a great tragedy in her life, but their childhood had been storybook perfect. A million miles away from bar fights and tattoos of naked mermaids.

"What are you thinking about?"

His sleep-roughened voice made her jump. She scrambled to recover her wits under his watchful gaze. A gaze that suggested Reed, too, was surprised to find himself asleep in her bed. "I was, uh...thinking maybe I'd get a tattoo. Something real bad, like a dragon eating a shark. Both of them on fire. And maybe the grim reaper standing in the background, for good measure. What do you think?"

"Anyone marks your skin, I put them in a world of hurt. That's what I think."

Julie tucked some stray hair behind her ear, trying to ignore the wave of fierce pleasure in her chest. His possessive attitude should bother her, confuse her. After all, why did he care what became of her once they parted ways? But she couldn't deny liking it. Craving more. "It was a joke. You always wake up this cranky?"

"You call this cranky?"

"What would you call it?"

"Honest."

Julie shook her head at him, still trying to gauge his mood. Taking a chance, she ran a finger along the scar at his hip, relieved when he didn't flinch under the tender touch. "Another bar fight?"

"No." He was silent a moment, tracking her movements closely. "Came by that one at home."

Her finger stilled, but apart from that, she showed zero reaction, afraid an ounce of pity on her face would cause him to shut down. "Your daddy do this to you?"

"I never called him that, but yes. With a broken Budweiser bottle."

She swallowed around the knot in her throat. "How old were you?"

"Twelve."

Julie's nature demanded she throw herself across his chest and wail to the heavens, but somehow she managed to keep her riotous emotions in check. While she'd been attending summer camp and hosting family barbecues, he'd been leading a pitiful existence. It made her sad. It horrified her. And it ticked her off good.

"How are you holding up down there, pixie? You look like you don't know whether to scream or break something."

"How would you feel about both?"

He shrugged his big shoulders. "It's your room."

She blew out a quick breath. "Do you want to tell me more?"

Brow furrowed, Reed glanced away. "Do you want to... know more?"

"Yes," Julie answered, before she could second-guess herself. Even knowing it wasn't wise. The more she learned about Reed, the more she understood him. Saw past his defenses. She was making it infinitely harder on herself by learning about the man beneath, but simply couldn't help it. At that moment, lying together in the dark, barriers didn't exist between them. She rested her head on the pillow and waited.

Reed didn't speak for a full minute. "I didn't call him daddy. I didn't call him anything, really. *Him*, I suppose. *You*. Never really used my name either, took to calling me *boy* after my mother passed." He tore his gaze away from her. "He took her in for a chemo treatment one afternoon. Next morning, she was just gone." Staring into space, he ran an absent hand through his hair. "About a week later, I came across Colton and Brock at the lake. I'd spent the night in Colton's boat—a few nights, actually. He didn't mention it, just asked if I wanted to go fishing."

Julie's throat felt closed; her eyes burned, nose tingled. She buried her face in the pillow as the image of a world-weary little boy belonging for the first time swam in her head. She wanted to go back in time and weep all over that little boy. Make him a sandwich. Clean him up. That very boy had grown into a man who carried around the damage, but she couldn't comfort the man. He wouldn't let her. She tried to hide her distress, but it escaped in a watery sob. "Did you catch anything?"

Laughter rumbled in his chest. "Couple of catfish."

She wailed even harder.

"Ah, Jesus. Come over here." Reed propped himself against the headboard and pulled her onto his lap, tucking her head under his chin. She was too upset to be surprised. "Go ahead and say it."

"Bless your little *hearts*."

He sighed. "There it is."

"Reed?"

"Huh, baby?"

"Your daddy not calling you by your name? It's not the

same thing as you not calling me Julie. It just isn't. Don't you go thinking about it one second more."

...

Reed couldn't speak for a long moment as he looked down at the weeping blonde who'd all but wrapped herself around his middle. *Exactly where she belongs.* He liked having her there. Loved it, actually. It felt vital. Necessary. Like if someone tried to pull her off of him, they would drag part of him away with her. And fuck, for the first time in his life, he was scared shitless.

"All right, Julie," he rasped into her hair, not knowing what else to say. Afraid if he opened his mouth, something would come out to send her away. Or keep her close. Either option unnerved him. He'd woken up to the best feeling of his life, his girl tucked into his chest where he could keep her safe. His first thought had been her name. *Julie.* The next had been, *what the hell is wrong with you?* He'd known going in that their relationship could only be temporary. Hell, temporary was all he did. More than one night with a woman was usually a stretch for him.

That feeling. That heavy dread when she'd run away from him that first night. The possessiveness he'd felt when she set her sights on Golden Boy. He should have known then. After spending a handful of minutes with her, he'd already been infatuated. Now that he knew her, had witnessed her compassion, knew the reasons behind her faults, he couldn't walk away. It was simply too late. If someone tried to take her away, God help them. He would fight them tooth and nail.

At the same time, however, he feared disaster. She'd devoted her life to making other people happy. He didn't give a flying shit about anyone else's feelings...save hers. He had a darkness inside him that could eclipse her goodness so easily. He pictured himself at Sunday dinner, breaking bread with her richer-than-sin family, and nearly laughed out loud. They would be horrified at their daughter's choice in men. That's if she chose him at all.

Panic threatened. He needed to consider the possibility that she still intended to walk away at the end of the week, free and clear of him. Why wouldn't she? He couldn't offer her a damn thing. All he had to barter with was himself. Julie could do better. She probably had wealthy men breaking down her door, if not for her sweet disposition and bombshell looks alone, then the security and connections her family provided. He had a decent savings account, more than comfortable for a man in his early thirties, but his sparse one-bedroom apartment in downtown Atlanta left a lot to be desired. Her future was bright. He would only dim it. He should walk away now and let it unfold the way it was supposed to. Let Julie have her emotionally undamaged husband and two blond babies.

Over his dead, lifeless body. Reed pulled her tighter against his chest, grunting his pleasure when she clung tighter, making him feel invincible.

"We need to talk, pixie—"

Her phone buzzed on the side table, startling her. She reached for it with a gasp. "Twenty missed calls. And...oh my Lord, it's almost four in the morning. I had no idea."

"Whatever it is can wait until daylight."

Reed cursed when she ignored him and answered the

phone. "Mrs. Anderson, well aren't you a night owl? Or is it an early bird? What did you need, sweetheart?" Her eyebrows rose. "A wake-up call at eight? Have you contacted the—" She nodded through a long pause. "Oh, you *did* request one with the front desk, too…well, you are one hundred and fifty percent right, Mrs. Anderson. You can't be too careful. Don't want to put all your eggs in one basket. One of them is bound to break. You get your beauty rest, now. Kiss Mr. Anderson for me if he's still awake, bless his heart. Good night, now."

Her hand shook as she disconnected and frantically began taking notes while listening to her voice mail messages. Reed frowned. He knew she liked to be efficient, but something about her reaction seemed off.

"Hey." He reached over and tried to pry the phone out of her hand. "*Julie.*"

She looked right through him. "Yes?"

"You can't save the world right now. It's almost morning—" Reed broke off as a possible reason for her abrupt attitude change occurred to him. Almost morning. She'd grown upset after noting the time. Unusually upset. The only other instance he could remember her losing her composure this way was that night in the forest. When they'd been talking about… "Is today the day? Serena…?"

"Yes," she snapped. "Yes, and as usual, I was off in my own world. Not sparing her a thought."

"That's ridiculous." He sat forward, plucked the pen from her hand. "You deserve to sleep. You can resume your candidacy for sainthood at a decent hour."

"Give it back."

Her cell phone buzzed in her hand. "Don't answer that."

Defiantly, she raised it to her ear. "Kady?"

Reed rolled his eyes when she slipped out of bed. Phone wedged between her ear and her shoulder, she pulled a thong out of her suitcase and slipped it on, the white material nestling perfectly at the center of her ass. Just like that, his cock grew hard. The idea of ripping off her lily-white thong and dragging her underneath him was almost too tempting to deny. He'd banish the memory of her twenty phone calls or her misplaced sense of responsibility to return them. If he didn't see the grief written all over her face, he wouldn't be hesitating.

"When was the last time someone saw Christine? Wait, Tyler is missing, too? Were they together?" Reed raised an eyebrow at her, but she held up a finger for silence. He watched as her gaze tracked down his chest to the erection lying across his belly. Her breath caught, nipples hardening. She seemed to remember her state of undress then, and hurriedly donned a bra and T-shirt. He felt a flash of satisfaction that her voice sounded raw when next she spoke. "Of course I'll help find them. Yes, of course I understand. We can't leave them missing. I'll take the trails…"

"Like hell," Reed mouthed from the bed.

"Call me if they show up. We'll all meet in the lobby after they're safe." Julie selected a pair of pants from her chest of drawers and wiggled them up over her hips, setting his teeth on edge. The longer it took her to get dressed, the more he became convinced she was teasing him on purpose. "Relax, sweetie. I'm sure they didn't get eaten by a bear. Christine is smart, you know that. If anything, she'd just interview him into early hibernation."

Reed swung his legs over the side of the bed and pulled

on his jeans. He added his black T-shirt just as Julie hung up with Kady. "I gather Christine and Tyler are missing?"

She sat down to lace up her sneakers. "No one has seen them since the scavenger hunt."

"Did anyone stop to consider they *want* to be missing?"

Julie scoffed. "Tyler wouldn't…not with Christine. He's all protective of her, like…oh."

"Right." He finished tying his boots and stood. "So we bust in like some kind of vigilante cock blocks and ruin their night. Sounds like a stellar plan."

Her eyes narrowed dangerously. "I know I sound like a broken record, but once again, no one is forcing you to come."

"Do you actually expect me to let you go bumbling around on a dark mountain by yourself?"

"*Bumbling?*"

"After you." Reed merely yanked open the door and gestured for her to proceed before him into the hallway. He knew his attitude bordered on shitty, but he couldn't summon the ability to care. He'd been seconds from exposing his feelings, *himself*, to Julie and once again she was worrying about everyone but herself. Apparently, he was the only one worried about *her*.

Chapter Fourteen

Julie trudged up the path, flashlight clenched tightly in her hand. She hadn't said a word to Reed since leaving her room and until now, he'd wisely stayed silent. As they ventured farther from the well-lit section of the resort, however, he'd moved closer. Began grunting, steadying her with a hand on her elbow whenever she made a misstep. Frustration radiated from every line of his body, mirroring her own, she was certain. Not only was her frustration intensified by his refusal to understand the need to find her missing best friend, Julie had to admit that some of her irritation was of a sexual nature. Seeing Reed sprawled out in her bed, taking up the majority of it with his painfully masculine body, fully aroused…it had taken every ounce of her willpower not to climb on top of him and take him inside of her. Forget everything and everyone a while longer and simply, but powerfully, fulfill their needs. Needs that were apparently endless and growing in strength by the moment.

Just feeling his concentrated gaze following her from his reclined position on the bed, she'd been subconsciously putting on a show for him. Bending forward more than necessary to find clothing in her suitcase, remaining topless longer than needed. Shameless behavior that she hadn't even been aware of at the time. She'd practically begged for him to drag her back to bed. And *damn* him, he hadn't. It was childish and unlike her in so many ways. Until recently. When he'd awoken some insatiable part of her that demanded satisfaction.

She didn't understand what was taking place inside her. Just the knowledge that Reed walked behind her, had his eyes trained on her, made Julie's body feel heated, ready, anxious. It wouldn't leave her. No matter how hard she tried to focus on the problem at hand. If it were purely physical, Julie felt confident she could control it. So close on the heels of having him open up to her, granting her a peek into his past, his abrasive attitude hurt twice as much. It made her want to end the fling now to save herself heartache later. His lack of understanding over her need to help when people needed her had only driven home the fact that they would never work.

It also made her want to cling tight and beg him not to let her go. To yell and rail and shake him until he decided to keep her. What sense did that make? Dread rose in her chest, mingling with self-disgust. She was being *that* girl. The fix-him girl, the *maybe-he-just-hasn't-found-the-right-woman* girl. Stupid. He didn't want to be fixed. He didn't want *one* girl. He'd never pretended otherwise and she'd proceeded accordingly, going into this with zero expectations. When had that changed? When had the prospect of parting ways started to inspire restless anxiety?

Lost in her turbulent thoughts, Julie's sneaker slipped off the edge of the path and she stumbled. Reed grasped her biceps and hauled her up against his chest before she could fall.

"Slow down and watch where you're going. You're going to break your goddamn ankle."

"Let go of me." With the heels of her hands, Julie pushed at his unyielding chest, but even she acknowledged her halfhearted attempt to get away. As if magnetized, her lower body pressed intimately against his, writhing closer under the pretense of freeing herself. Reed's eyes narrowed suspiciously in the near-darkness. He wrenched the flashlight out of her hands and dropped it on the path.

"I can't tell if you're struggling because you want me to let you go, or if you want to be overpowered. Explain yourself, Julie."

Her panting breaths were her only answer. She curled a leg around his waist and gave another hard push against his solid wall of muscle. Contradicting herself once more. Between her thighs, she felt Reed harden in reaction to whatever he perceived on her face. He made a desperate sound. "Answer me. Let you go? Or drag you down to the ground and fuck you on your hands and knees? I need an answer now."

Her pulse raced. She could hear it roaring in her ears. Using his shoulders for support, she hitched herself higher and wrapped both legs around his waist. "Fuck me."

"*Thank Christ.*" Reed's hands gripped her bottom tight. His mouth devoured hers with a groan as he leaned back and let her feel the full force of his need. They kissed frantically,

Julie digging her fingers into his hair, meeting his potent kiss head-on. He twisted her hair in his fist and pulled her head back. His mouth raced over her neck, biting and sucking as she moaned.

The rough treatment, while exactly what she needed, craved…it jostled something inside of her. Shook it loose. Her uncertainty. The inevitability of losing him. Losing *this*.

She buried her face in his neck, heard herself sob once, loudly. "I don't know who I am with you. I don't understand who I turn into."

Reed stilled. She knew from his unsteady breaths the effort it cost him to stop, so her arms tightened around him automatically in a comforting gesture. When he flinched at the action, horrible, jagged pain sliced through her chest. After everything, the way they'd opened up to each other, it felt almost like a betrayal. Out of self-preservation, she scrambled out of his arms.

He tried to tighten his hold, but it was too late. His irritated curse echoed through the woods. "You want to know who you are with me? Maybe you're finally being *yourself*. You stop worrying about pleasing everyone else and finally focus on pleasing Julie." He swiped an impatient hand through his hair. "Maybe you stop trying to be your sister for a goddamn minute."

The words had barely left his mouth before Julie started backing away, gulping air into her lungs. It felt as though she'd been hit in the stomach with a two-by-four. She backed away, holding up a hand when he came toward her. "H-how dare…you? Who do you think you are?"

"I didn't mean it to come out like that."

"But you meant it," she sputtered. "About me trying to

be Serena."

His next words were low and punctuated. "This people-pleasing bullshit…it's going to take a toll on you, Julie. It'll never be enough. You can't live up to a memory. No one can."

Her insides shook at his words. She refused to recognize the possible truth behind them. A truth that had never occurred to her. It hurt to think about it, so she struck back the only way she could to keep the thoughts at bay. "You don't get to diagnose *me*. Not when you're such a mess yourself. You flinch when I hug you. You hide in your dark corner, scaring everyone off who might actually talk to you."

"You're right." He shrugged stiffly. "I'm fucked up. At least I admit it."

"And that makes it okay?" Needing to occupy her hands, she snatched the flashlight off the ground. "I'd rather make people happy. I'd rather people feel comfortable coming to me for help than alienate everyone. Keeping everyone at arm's length because I'm terrified to be happy."

He crossed his arms over his chest. "I guess that's where we differ."

"Oh, I can think of at least a thousand ways we differ." She felt the pressing need to lash out at him. To make him hurt as badly as she did in that moment. Not only had he taken the trust she'd shown him and used it to expose her as a fraud, but now he couldn't be acting more coldhearted if he tried. Right when she needed him most, she could see him turning to stone in front of her eyes, and she wanted to watch that wall crumble to the ground. "Looks like I really did walk into the wrong room that first night, huh?"

His whole body jerked. "*Take it back.*"

"Don't hold your breath."

Voices approached, shattering the strained silence. Loud, arguing voices. One of which Julie immediately recognized as Christine. Relief and disappointment warred within her. Relief that her friend was safe and unharmed. Disappointment that this scene between them still felt unfinished. What would he have said next? What would he have done to convince her to take the statement back? Ridiculous, pointless thoughts that wouldn't matter now that he'd painted the forest with her insecurities. Told her how he really saw her. This bitter, unsatisfying ending had been inevitable. She'd just had a ton of bricks dropped on her head, having Serena's ghost thrown in her face on today of all days. Perhaps it was best if they left the ending unspoken. She simply couldn't suffer one more blow.

Julie turned in the direction of the voices and started walking. "I'm done talking about this."

He laughed darkly. "We're not done until you take back what you said."

She scoffed. "I think your ego is large enough to survive one tiny blow." Hearing him closing in on her, she picked up her pace. "This has been a god-awful waste of time."

"Walked into the wrong room, Julie?" His arm snaked around her belly, stopping her in her tracks. When he pulled her back against his wall of strength, she felt herself begin to melt, but somehow kept her posture rigid. He only held her tighter, molding himself to her back. His breath fanned over her neck as he spoke. "How fast do you think I can prove you wrong?"

"Let me go," she said through clenched teeth, struggling with enough effort that he had no choice but to free her or risk injuring her. As soon as she regained her balance, she whirled on him. "I have no doubt you could prove, once again, that I'm attracted to you. It's what comes afterward. The *nothing* that comes afterward that matters. You're not *capable* of anything more. So just...walk away, Reed."

If she blinked, she would have missed the stricken look that flashed in his face. Just as quickly, though, it was gone and replaced with his signature granite countenance. It made her want to stomp and scream at him to get the first reaction back. At least it would prove this thing between them had meant something.

"Nothing was ever supposed to come afterward," he said woodenly. "I never claimed I could give that to you."

Christine came into view then, being carried down the path by Tyler. They both looked incredibly annoyed, leaves and forest debris clinging to their clothing and hair. When she saw Christine wince in pain, concern for her friend trumped all else and Julie walked away from Reed, who looked frozen to the spot.

"What happened?"

Christine opened her mouth to reply, but Tyler spoke first, his green eyes flashing angrily. "Ankle sprain."

She ignored Reed's weary sigh behind her and went into fix-it mode. Relief, she was ashamed to admit, spread in her belly at having something to focus on beside the man burning holes into her back. "Oh, you poor thing. Let's get you back to the resort right now. Ice and elevation, that's what you need. We'll get it fixed up real good. Don't you worry, sweetheart. I'm going to have room service bring you up a big old cup of coffee and some chocolate. Aunt Sylvie always said there's nothing you can't cure with chocolate and time." She patted Tyler on the arm, but he didn't take his eyes off Christine. "Can you carry her the rest of the way or should—"

"I've got her."

Christine's fist balled up. "I ca—"

"I said I *got* it," Tyler snapped, looking as though he'd take on anyone who made the mistake of removing Christine from his arms. "Julie, you can go lead the way with Reed, since you have the flashlight."

Julie nodded, mentally registering the fact that Reed had definitely been onto something. Enough sparks were flying between these two to start a fire. An ill-advised endeavor in the forest. "Fabulous. Let's get moving." Feeling Reed's steady gaze on her and refusing to meet it, she pulled her cell phone out of her pocket and dialed Kady. "The redheaded eagle has landed. We'll meet y'all in the lobby."

Chapter Fifteen

Reed leaned against the wall in the lobby and watched Julie command the troops. Even at the early hour, she'd managed to rally several members of the resort staff to their cause. Arranging room service, finding a pair of crutches in the stockroom, borrowing medical supplies from the infirmary for Tyler to utilize in treating Christine. The bridal party, bleary-eyed and haphazardly dressed, stood in a semicircle around her, waiting for their marching orders.

Tyler had long since disappeared with Christine, silently carrying her down the hallway toward her room. Kady and Colton, propped up against each other, looked exhausted.

Everyone, everything, functioned normally around him, while inside, he felt ripped to shreds. Having steeled himself at a young age against feeling too many emotions, it blew his mind that no one could see his misery. It felt as though it should be painted in bright red across his chest. Once again, he'd had Julie in his arms, holding his pitiful, broken body against hers. For a brief second in time, he'd felt healed. Redeemed. Then he'd said something unforgivable. As if some subconscious, terrified part of him wanted to drive her away, when consciously, all he wanted was to crush her to him. Absorb her scent. Her light. Never let her go.

Brock, wearing beat-up jeans and a Braves hat, threw himself into a nearby leather recliner, tossing an amused glance at Reed. "You can't stare her into liking your ass."

"Shut it."

"All right." He yanked his cap down lower. "Too tired to argue, anyhow."

Julie's chipper voice reached him. "We're going to need flats for all the bridesmaids. We can't have Christine being the odd one out. Preferably silver to match the dresses. Who wants to take that on?" She glanced around curiously. "Where's Regan? I need my shopping expert."

Reed had never seen Brock move so fast. He leaped out of the chair, waving a hand at Julie. "I'll find her. Silver shoes. Got it. Anything else?"

"N-no. Thank you, Brock." She patted him on the shoulder and gave him a smile that had Reed grinding his molars. *I never make her smile. Only cry or get angry. Or both.* "Bless your heart. I'm sure Regan can figure out sizes."

Reed shook his head as Brock asked for Regan's room number, then all but sprinted from the lobby. Apparently they'd all drunk the Kool-Aid. He switched his attention back to Julie. She and Kady were debating the idea of canceling dance rehearsal that afternoon.

Kady blew out a breath. "Knowing Christine, she's embarrassed enough as it is. Canceling will only make it worse."

Julie pursed her lips and nodded. "You're right. We'll just get her a big comfy chair to sit in and watch. It'll keep her involved. We can all take turns sitting with her." She returned her attention to the group. "Okay, I'm going to go check on the patient. You can all go back to sleep now. Does anyone need anything?"

Half the group groaned in relief and turned to leave; the other half began lobbing requests at Julie, which she dutifully wrote down on a notepad. Reed couldn't watch it another second. She looked dead on her feet, today marked the anniversary of her sister's death, and unless she'd sneaked in a meal during the hour they'd been apart the evening prior, she hadn't had anything to eat in damn near twenty-four hours.

The haunted look he'd put in her eye with his insensitive comments still hadn't dimmed and it made him want to rage at everyone to leave her the hell alone. To do so, he suspected, would only push her further away. If such a thing were at all possible. He'd done a bang-up job of driving her squarely out of his reach, and his interference would not be welcome.

Jaw grinding, he propelled himself off the wall and strode out the back door of the lobby, uncertain of where he was headed and not giving a shit if he ended up in China.

"Whoa. Wait up, buddy." Reed turned to find Colton jogging after him, hands shoved in his pockets to ward off the morning cold. "Where you headed?"

"Shouldn't you be in bed with your bride?"

"Yeah. I figure there'll be plenty of time for that once I get the ring on her finger, though." He matched Reed's pace on the path snaking through the resort village, but didn't say anything as they walked. Reed knew his friend well enough to recognize his game. The advantages of knowing someone since childhood meant understanding how their mind worked.

Colton probably figured if he stayed silent long enough, Reed would cave and explain why he'd stormed off. In his current mood, he didn't feel like giving even Colton the satisfaction of reading him so well, but as always, he remembered the role Colton played in getting him through those early years. Hell, half the reason he was alive was walking beside him. He'd vowed never to forget that.

For the first time since he could remember, Reed attempted to put his feelings into words, ignoring the way Colton's steps faltered on the path when he started talking.

"So is this how it always is? You need to…suffer in order to gain something?" He cleared his throat uncomfortably. "My father kicks me out and I'm sleeping on a boat. But in the end, it's how I meet you and Brock." Brow furrowed, Colton stayed silent beside him. *Bastard.* "Then it takes me nearly dying from a stab wound to turn it all around. Join the academy. And now this"—he blew out a harsh breath—"this *girl*, she's making me suffer, too. Even when I *have* her, I'm suffering over the idea of *not* having her. I'd take the stab wound again to stop it."

"Don't tempt fate."

"Oh, he speaks."

"I was getting there." Colton turned away, but Reed caught his smile and made a sound of disgust in response. "So if I'm hearing you correctly, this girl makes you want to get yourself stabbed."

"This is why I don't talk much."

Colton laughed. "All right, I'll be serious. Keep going."

"You were expecting more?" Reed sighed. "You two idiots? I had no problem figuring out. The academy was physical work. That, I understood, no problem. With Julie…" He shook his head. "On the surface, I know anything between us is impossible. But I think it might be twice as impossible for me to stay away. To…let her walk."

"First of all…the girl is Julie?"

Reed nodded once.

"Maid of honor. Nice." He offered his hand out for a fist bump, which Reed ignored. "Why is it impossible?"

Reed snorted, but Colton merely raised an eyebrow. "Remember that summer Brock's mother played the *Phantom of the Opera* soundtrack nonstop? Just on a constant loop. Morning until night. Then she made us sit with her and watch the old black-and-white movie version?"

"Pure, unadulterated torture."

"Right. Well Julie is Christine and I'm the Phantom. Minus the mask."

"And the singing ability."

"Fine. You get what I'm saying."

"I get it, sure." Colton shrugged. "I just don't agree."

Reed grunted. "People would wonder what the hell she's doing with me."

"Since when do you give a damn what people think? And by the way, everyone wants Christine to end up with the Phantom. They're soul mates, man."

"I'm beginning to regret this metaphor."

The two friends walked in silence for a moment. "Have to say, I never expected to find myself on a romantic morning walk with Reed Lawson. Discussing musical theater of all things."

"Well, congratulations. You can cross it off your bucket list." He shot Colton a look. "And quit smiling."

Colton barked a laugh. "Final word of advice before I leave you to commune with nature." He pulled Reed to a stop. "Don't leave anything unsaid. Women might *say* they like mysterious men, but that's only in the beginning. Soon enough, they start *hating* the mystery. They want what you're thinking translated into three different languages." He took a deep breath. "Tell her what you're thinking. Doesn't matter if you think it sounds stupid. Just get it out there. Hell, sometimes it's even the right thing. And when that happens…" Colton slapped him on the shoulder. "It's like Christmas morning and Super Bowl Sunday wrapped up in one."

Reed hid his amusement. "Who could pass that up?"

"Exactly." Colton glanced over his shoulder. "I better head back. Kady is probably looking for me."

"Don't keep her waiting, then."

"Oh, I won't." Colton started back in the direction they came. After a few steps, he stopped. "Hey Reed." He appeared to be searching for the right words. "When you think she deserves someone better? When you can't imagine being the one who actually gets to keep her? That's how you know *you're* the one who deserves her. Not some asshole in a puffy shirt carrying a sword."

"This conversation never took place."

Colton jogged backward down the path singing "Think of Me," Brock's mother's favorite song from the *Phantom* soundtrack. Reed flipped him the bird, but as soon as Colton disappeared from view, he couldn't help but laugh under his breath.

...

Julie raised a hand to knock on Christine's door just as it opened and a resigned-looking Tyler exited. She started to ask him if everything was all right, then thought better of it. Obviously, something had gone wrong between the two. Best not to pry. Or get involved and make it worse.

"Tyler, is there anything I can do for you? You look downright exhausted and no wonder. Carrying Christine like a bona fide hero through the woods. I'd imagine you're about ready to drop."

He gave a halfhearted attempt at a smile, but there was an unholy suffering in his eyes. "I'm fine, really."

She patted him on the arm. "I'll make sure she's all right. Go take care of yourself."

"Will you call me if she needs me? Or pretends she doesn't, but really does?"

"Absolutely."

Tyler hesitated, but turned and left. Julie watched him walk off, obviously under the weight of a heavy heart. She understood how he felt. Since her and Reed's argument in the woods, she'd been burdened by a yawning, empty feeling in her stomach. Watching him disappear from the lobby had only made it worse. While she felt certain her actions were for the best, it didn't stop the dull, insistent ache from spreading the longer she went without seeing him. If anything, the churning feeling should strengthen her resolve. If she felt this terrible after only a few days with Reed, allowing their affair to last through the week would prove infinitely worse. The assurance did nothing to quash the urge to go find him.

Apologize for her harsh parting words. Apologize for saying one thing and communicating another with her body. For everything.

Attempting to focus, Julie pushed the door open and slipped inside. Christine lay on the bed, ankle propped on a pillow, one arm flung over her eyes.

"I told you to leave," she said tearfully.

Julie winced. "Hey, sweetie. It's just me."

"Oh." Christine quickly swiped at her eyes. "Hey, Julie. Come on in."

"If this is a bad time—"

"No!" Eyes toward the ceiling, she blew out a shaky breath. "Actually, I could really use the company. I feel like such a clumsy idiot. Anything you can do to take my mind off this would be much appreciated."

She held up a white box and shook it. "Fudge squares?"

"Bingo."

Julie sank down on the end of the bed and toed her shoes off. "Truth be told, even world-class athletes sprain their ankles, Christine. And they don't look half as good doing it."

"I was distracted," she mumbled around a fudge square. "And stupid."

"I can relate."

"Reed as difficult as he looks?"

Her head whipped around. "Why do you assume—oh, forget it. Everyone knows, don't they?"

Christine responded by popping another piece of fudge into her mouth.

Julie debated for a moment over whether or not to disclose the entire story to Christine. *If you can't tell your best friend you've fallen for an impossible man who spanks your lady parts, who can you tell?*

She sent Christine a sly smile. "Remember that guy in college? Bobby Cox was his name. He brought me flowers and took me for a helicopter ride on our second date. Brought along wine and had the pilot play a Norah Jones CD to get me in a kissing mood. Remember?"

Christine sighed dreamily. "Political science major. Blond. Yeah, I remember."

She dropped the smile. "Well, this is nothing like that."

"Oh."

"Yeah. Reed doesn't do the woo. I'd hazard to guess that he doesn't even know who Norah Jones is."

Mouth full, Christine sadly shook her head.

"Uh-huh." Julie picked at the comforter. "He doesn't compliment. Or try to find things we have in common. He doesn't ask. He takes." She thought about the way he'd made sure she got something to eat after the party at Spago. The way he'd cleaned up so she wouldn't have to. His refusal to let her search alone in the dark woods. "But when he does make an effort, even just the smallest thing"—*like chanting my name until his voice goes hoarse, taking me to that hot spring*—"it blows Bobby Cox and his Norah Jones CD out of the water."

She glanced over to find Christine studying her. Wordlessly, her friend handed her the box of fudge, which she gratefully accepted.

"Can I ask you a question, Christine?"

"You know you can."

Julie hesitated. "Am I different? Since Serena…?"

Christine tilted her head, eyes full of sympathy. "You're the same person, Julie. The same person with different priorities."

Absorbing that, she nodded. "Right."

"What brought this on?" Christine's eyes widened. "Oh God. Today…"

"Don't worry about it," Julie rushed to say. "And please, don't remind any of the girls. This week is about Kady." She patted Christine's arm when she nodded reluctantly. "Anyway, the anniversary is only partially responsible. Reed said…he thinks I'm overcompensating for Serena's absence. Trying to *be* her."

Her friend paled. That's when Julie knew there'd been some truth behind his words. Why had no one ever said anything? How could she not have seen it?

She shifted uncomfortably on the bed. "Guess he was right."

"No. Not entirely." Christine exhaled on a sigh. "But we all worry you take on too much." She laid her hand over Julie's. "I don't know Reed. But is it possible he said it out of concern? You've been working yourself to the bone. It's hard for the people who care about you to ignore."

"He doesn't…it's not like that with us. It's sex. Plain and simple."

"Julie." Christine pursed her lips. "Give me some credit. I'm an investigative journalist. When that man is around you, he looks like he doesn't know whether to kiss you breathless or tie you to a chair so you will finally relax." She laughed at Julie's stunned expression. "Does he want to jump your bones? Yes. But for my money? He wants more than inappropriate activities involving a ladder."

She gasped. "How did you know about that?"

"I didn't. I suspected it when I interrupted you two. You

just confirmed my hunch."

"How come you haven't won a Pulitzer yet?"

Christine smirked. "All in good time."

Feeling slightly better, even though she still had *a lot* to think about, Julie flopped back on the bed. She didn't believe Christine's assessment of Reed, but she needed to stop thinking about him for now. Against her will, she'd let herself develop some seriously complicated feelings for a man who saw her faults way too easily. One who would leave her behind at the earliest opportunity. She spoke around the lump in her throat. "Your turn. What had Tyler walking out of here like a scolded toddler?

Christine stared off into space. "It's a long, long story."

"I've got time."

Chapter Sixteen

Well heck, Julie thought, surveying the nearly silent bridal party in the ballroom. Where was Reed? Rain and howling wind battered the floor-to-ceiling windows, putting a damper on the already-gloomy mood inside and preventing escape to the outdoors. The atmosphere was so thick, if you tried to cut it with a knife, the knife would get good and stuck. Leaving you weaponless. Sort of how she felt at the moment. Defenseless, unsure of herself. Anxious.

Would Reed show up to dance rehearsals or blow it off? Just the thought of seeing him made her pulse pound, even as she dreaded coming face-to-face with him after their last encounter. Seeing the judgment on his face. The pity. Perhaps she'd see none of it. Only the evidence that he'd mentally moved on.

Which would be worse? At this point, Julie couldn't tell. Nor could she allow herself to think about it another second. Pigs would fly before she spent the anniversary of Serena's death obsessing over a stubborn, unavailable man. Four years ago today, when she'd received the call that would forever be seared into her brain, she'd been on the way to hang banners at a pep rally for the football team, deciding which postgame party to attend, wondering if her butt looked fat from certain angles in the mirror. So frivolous. Pointless. She wouldn't be that girl again. Worrying about things she couldn't change. Reed was one of those things.

Julie took a fortifying breath and surveyed the room. Apparently she and Reed weren't the only ones who'd quarreled. Christine and Tyler were having a hushed, seemingly tense conversation on the far side of the room, Regan was pointedly ignoring Brock, and Sophie—well, damn, she'd gone and dressed herself up like a rebellious preacher's daughter. She looked dynamite. Julie raised her eyebrows when she saw Logan take careful notice of the transformation. Kady and Colton entered the room laughing, but their steps faltered as the obvious tension rolled over them, too.

"Uh...good evening?" Kady said hesitantly.

Julie swallowed her nerves as Francois entered the ballroom behind the smitten couple, saving them from an uncomfortable silence when no one responded to the bride-to-be's greeting. A middle-aged man with obviously dyed jet-black hair, Francois's every movement appeared planned, elegant. With a flutter of his fingers, he waved without looking to the sullen group and crossed to Julie, whom he'd correctly guessed—probably from the huge smile plastered to her face—was in charge. Hopefully he couldn't tell her face felt seconds from crumbling. She'd planned this wedding to perfection, wanting it to be beautiful and memorable for her friend. Yet judging from the mood, everyone seemed hellbent on ruining it. After Reed calling her out in the forest, even *she* was questioning her own motivation. Did she enjoy the exhaustive planning or was she punishing herself? No time to think about it now.

"Monsieur!" Julie added extra wattage to her smile and held out her hand, which the dance instructor shook once, inclining his head. "As you can tell, we are so excited to begin. Been looking forward to this for days, in fact."

She politely ignored the snort leveled from Regan's direction.

Francois nodded, giving everyone a critical once-over. "Right, then. So *this* is what I'm working with." He pinched the bridge of his nose and sighed. "Everyone get a partner. Your hour has begun and we must not waste anyone's time. Mine especially."

Everyone shifted uncomfortably, unsure of who to partner with. When an impatient Francois clapped his hands loudly, Regan strolled over to Logan, put her hand on his shoulder, and sent him a dazzling smile, which he eventually returned, if slightly less enthusiastic. Tyler whispered something to Christine and helped her to the dance floor. Gaze still fixed on Regan, Brock held out a hand to Sophie, who gratefully accepted.

It struck Julie that she didn't have a partner. Reed still hadn't walked through the door. Francois was busy walking around, correcting everyone's posture. She'd just have to learn the dance visually. Julie backed away from the group until she connected with the wall, leaning against it. She would not let this upset her. She would *not*. Tears threatened under her eyelids nonetheless. Tears that had nothing to do with dance lessons, prickly instructors, or feuding friends. Things that would normally get under her skin so deep she wouldn't rest until she righted them. Instead, she encountered sorrow for her sister, self-pity for herself, anger toward Reed for dredging up all these emotions, then leaving her to drown in them. It all rose to the surface, pulling her under. Thankfully, everyone appeared too caught up in their own situation to notice her smile finally fall prey to the pressure.

Julie had no idea how long she stood there, watching the proceedings without actually seeing them. After catching one or two worried glances in her direction, she'd zoned out. Numbed by grief and confusion over too many feelings at once. She'd spent too long fixing everyone else. Now she had no idea how to fix herself.

Angry whispering, coming from Christine and Tyler, snapped her out of her daze. Swallowing her emotions, she started forward, intent on mediating the argument before it disrupted the lesson. Kady beat her to it. She pulled away from Colton with an irritated groan. Her arms encompassed the entire bridal party as she yelled, "What the hell is wrong with everyone?"

No one answered. With a muffled scream, Kady spun on her heel and slammed out of the ballroom, Sophie and a worried-looking Colton in her wake. Everyone stared at one another for a moment, then one by one began to disperse, beginning with an all-too-happy-to-bail Regan. Francois threw up his hands, muttering in French, and began to storm off. Julie, watching the disaster unfold with dawning horror, sprang into motion. She couldn't let some lover's spat ruin her best friends nuptials.

"Wait. We're not finished, you guys. You need to know

this dance for the reception." No one paid her any attention, all their focuses elsewhere. Julie targeted the instructor. "Francois—"

"Monsieur," he corrected her.

"Monsieur, please. Give me five minutes to straighten this out. I'll—"

He shook his head in disgust. "They are unteachable."

Julie was prepared to bribe him if necessary, but the instructor stomped out of the room before she could even open her mouth. One by one, everyone followed, some murmuring heartfelt apologies to her as they went. When she stood alone in the giant ballroom, she sank to the floor like a puppet.

Done. She was done. Every ounce of strain rushed to the fore until it felt like she was drowning. No matter how hard she tried, her efforts were never enough. Everyone could dance the Macarena at the reception for all she cared. If someone rustled up a limbo stick, she wouldn't even bat an eyelash. Obviously everyone would prefer that to a waltz. She flat-out didn't give a hoot anymore. What the hell was the point? She would never be good enough. Never be Serena.

I guess everyone is just going to have to settle for Julie. She hurled the clipboard across the room and took out a potted plant. "*Damnitshitheadbastardmotherfucker!*"

...

Reed sat at the hotel bar, a glass of whiskey untouched in front of him. Picking it up and bringing it to his lips seemed like too much of an effort. If he moved any part of himself, the numbness he'd managed to achieve would dissipate and the feelings would rush back in and overwhelm him. He'd missed the damn dance rehearsal. Completely blown it off and now he felt a dull, permeating sickness thinking of the implications of that. If he'd wanted to fix things with Julie, he'd just gone and royally fucked himself.

One minute, he'd been standing in his room ready to go, wearing a suit and everything. Might have even psyched himself up for a dance or two. Then he'd caught a glimpse of himself in the mirror on the way out. The next thing he knew, he was ordering a double whiskey, neat. One-Eyed Jack, no less, as if irony could be appreciated when he felt like he'd been run over by a semi truck. That suited man in the mirror wasn't him. It would *never* be him. Despite what Colton believed, he couldn't make a girl like Julie happy. She'd been right, back in the woods. He wasn't capable of *more*. Thanks to his past, he had no example to go on, either. Knowing her, she would work double time trying to give them a fighting chance. Watching her spin her wheels would make him miserable when nothing she did would be effective anyway.

He would be her biggest failure.

As a child, he'd seen firsthand what a damaged man could do to a woman. He'd watched his mother fade into nothing with each passing day at the abusive hands of his father. Back then, he'd been too young to do anything about it. He had no choice but to do something about it now. To let go of this ridiculous idea that Julie *belonged* to him and walk away. Ensure she didn't meet the same fate as his mother and leave her intact. Because God knew he was damaged—every scar on his body told that tale—while Julie went around doling out happiness to everyone she crossed paths with. If he dulled that part of her, he wouldn't be able to live with himself. Damn it, why hadn't he done this *before* he let himself consider the idea of keeping her? How could he bear it?

A perfectly manicured hand slapped down on the bar in front of him, rattling the cage he'd built around himself.

"Hey. Asshole."

He looked up into the face of one truly pissed-off Regan. Good, he'd love a fight. Anything to take away this horrible dread he couldn't shake. He turned in his stool and gave her an imposing look he usually reserved for his team. "Come again?"

Regan didn't so much as blink. "Oh, I think you heard me."

"No shit. I'm giving you a chance to rephrase."

She looked disgusted with him. *Join the club.* "You know, I really misjudged you, Reed. And I don't misjudge people. Ever." A glance toward the door. "Although apparently it's a week for firsts."

"Is there a point to this?"

"There's always a point when I'm talking." She actually poked him in the chest. "That first night, I saw something in you I thought would be good for my friend. I trusted my gut and switched that room key. You really let me down. Worse, you let the most genuine woman either one of us knows down."

Pain broke through the numbness. *I let her down. Fuck, I let her down.* "Then it looks like you both saw something that wasn't there. I never promised her anything. Do I look like the white picket fence type to you?"

"No. You look like a coward."

She looked a little surprised at her own outburst, but it didn't compare to the blast of anger he felt hearing the truthfulness behind that word. The anger was directed solely at himself. How he'd chosen to handle the situation. Running to a bar just like his father would have done. What sense did that make when he'd pushed Julie away so he wouldn't become his old man and ruin her? His actions had accomplished just that.

Regan wasn't finished, though. Part of him wanted her to keep going. Jesus, he deserved it. "This has been a waste of my time," she said. "Leaving her standing there all alone without a partner was the nail in your coffin. I'll never forgive you for what I saw on her face today."

The air left his lungs, a vicious pounding starting in his temples. He thought of his girl standing there watching everyone else dance, when she'd been the one to plan the whole damn thing, and he wanted to break something. Lots of somethings. Oh God, he'd been sitting here so mired in his own bullshit, he'd forgotten today was the anniversary of Serena's death. "Where is she? Is she okay?"

"Oh no, the Regan help line is hanging up now. You're on your own."

The words hadn't finished leaving Regan's mouth before Reed jumped to his feet. He needed to find Julie. Needed to touch her, to fix what he'd broken. This overwhelming anguish he felt at the idea of her in pain told him something important. It told him beyond a shadow of a doubt that he would kill himself making sure she never felt that way again by his hand. No matter what it took. Setting aside his demons, opening up about his past...hell, even cuddling. If she gave him a chance, he wouldn't screw it up. The alternative, living with the gaping emptiness he felt now, the emptiness *she'd* filled this week, wasn't a possibility anymore.

Before he could haul ass to Julie's room and demand to be let inside, he forced himself to slow down. He wasn't about to raid an Atlanta drug den, he was convincing a woman to let him love her. Shouting at her through a door wouldn't cut it. Not after how badly he'd failed.

How do you fix this, Reed? This time it counts.
Think.

• • •

An hour later, Reed took a slow, steadying breath and knocked on Julie's door. His determined knock echoed the one in his chest. In his line of work, getting through doors was what he did best. This might be his hardest job yet, because once he got through this door, he had another one to get through. And no amount of brute force or commands would work on the second one. He listened for movement on the other side and heard none. Before he could panic, a shadow moved across the peephole, disappearing just as quickly. Relief at having her so close turned to desperation when the door stayed shut.

"Pixie, let me in."

Her muffled sigh poured over him. "Please just leave. We've said everything that needed saying."

The finality in her voice almost sent him to his knees. "I haven't. Not by a damn sight. Open the door for me, baby."

Something hit the door. Her head, he suspected. "I'm trying to make this easy for you."

"Fuck easy."

"We're too different. This never would have worked."

Reed laid his palms flat on the door, his pulse kicking up a notch. "*Would* have worked, Julie?" Hope flared. Hope that he might have a chance. "Did you…had you considered it? Us?"

For long moments, all he got was silence. "Yes. I thought about how it would be a disaster. I thought about how you would belittle the things that I consider important. Just like you've done since the wedding started. All those events you ridiculed and made a joke out of? I planned them. It's what I do. It's what I'll always do, Reed. I make things pretty. And you hate pretty."

"Jesus, pixie…please, stop." He pinched the bridge of his nose. "I don't like hearing how I hurt you. That I…*would* hurt you. I don't like it."

To his utter shock, the door eased open. Julie stood framed by light, looking so fragile and beautiful he stopped breathing, afraid he might interrupt that beauty. There was more, though. She had fire in her eyes, as if she'd finally reached the end of her fraying rope. Damn it, he should have been there to catch her when it snapped. "Reed, if you came here to get me into bed, t-to prove some stupid point, you should know I've already taken out a potted plant today and I'm working my way up to something bigger. I—" Her gaze shot wide as it traveled down his body. "Why are you wearing a tuxedo?"

Jesus, he was sweating. At least he'd diverted her anger. "The bet we made. At the scavenger hunt." He relaxed slightly when recognition dawned on her face, followed by confusion. "I told you I won, which was true." His voice went husky, and he held out his hand. "I wouldn't trade the prize that followed for anything. But I consider making you happy the bigger win, Julie. I wanted to…show you that."

Julie stared at his outstretched hand for what seemed like an eternity. When she finally took it, cool, slim fingers slipped through his larger ones, locking them together. The stiffness in his shoulders relaxed just slightly. He wanted to pull her into his arms, but judging from her wary gaze, it would send her packing. It didn't stop the urge from gripping him. She looked stressed out. His body knew how to relieve that stress. His nature demanded he distract her from her troubles the only way he knew how. But his brain, and yeah, his heart, told him it wouldn't work this time.

Jesus, that scared the hell out of him.

Reed did his best to calm the rising fear as they walked past the lobby area and wound down another hallway. At the very end, he pushed open a heavy wooden door leading to the solarium he'd found earlier after his head-clearing walk. He breathed a mental sigh of relief to find it empty, save the plush furniture and bookcases full of reading material. Rain pelted the glass ceiling, the reason he'd specifically chosen this particular room to bring Julie. He closed the door behind them, locked it, and watched her wander through the room, taking it in. Even he, who admittedly didn't know a damn thing about romance, could appreciate the atmosphere. Soft lamplight, the smell of leather, no sound except the falling rain. Even so, her stiff posture remained. He took a deep breath and waited for her to see the blanket and deck of cards he'd laid out in front of the window.

Julie paused at the edge of the flannel. "What's this?"

"I…uh…" He crossed to her, sat down on the floor. "I thought we could play go fish. Since it's raining outside and all."

Reed could feel her staring at the top of his head, but he couldn't look up at her, instead busying himself shuffling the deck of cards he'd purchased at the gift shop. Damn it, he'd put himself out there with this plan. It could very well be all wrong. Who's to say she wanted to remember her sister this way? Doing something they, as sisters, had shared exclusively? Who's to say she wanted *him* to be a part of that? Reed braced for the worst, fearing her rejection. If she walked out now, he didn't know if he'd recover. So he waited. When she plopped down in front of him, shifting slowly into a cross-legged position, he couldn't prevent a tiny sigh of relief from escaping.

When he started to deal the cards, Julie stopped him with a hand on his. "Wait." Her voice sounded husky. "I have to cut the deck. With my eyes closed. It's tradition."

"Okay."

Their gazes locked for a heavy moment, before her eyelids slid down to cover the blue eyes he missed immediately. She lifted the top half of the deck, nodding to indicate he should place the bottom half over it, which Reed did before taking back the deck. He didn't take his eyes off her the entire time. Couldn't. She looked so incredibly soft sitting in the dim light, shadows cast by the swaying trees outside playing over her face. With her dress spread out around her on the floor, looking like something out of a fairy tale, it took every ounce of Reed's willpower not to drag her across the blanket. As a child, he'd never had quiet moments like this. It struck him then that while he'd arranged this for her, to commemorate the anniversary of Serena's passing, it seemed to be filling some long-empty void inside him as well.

"You're not allowed to let me win. Serena always let me win."

Reed thought for a moment. "How do you throw a game of go fish? It all depends on the cards you're dealt."

Julie picked up the cards Reed tossed in front of her. "She'd ask me for cards she knew I didn't have. Cards she already held, I suppose. I'd tell her to 'go fish' so many times, she'd have her whole hand full after five turns. I'd always run out first." She smoothed her hand over the blanket. "I knew the whole time, but I never said anything. I liked winning. Isn't that silly? Two girls sitting there, playing a pointless game when the outcome had already been determined?"

When her breath hitched on the last word, he knew she was rambling to hide her emotions. Again, he quashed the need to comfort physically and focused on what she'd said. "It's not silly. You were both giving each other what you needed. The game was just an excuse to accomplish that."

Julie frowned, shook her head. "I'm the one who got to win. What did Serena get out of it?"

"She got to spend time with you." Her eyes widened in a way Reed couldn't interpret. The reaction made him want to backpedal. Make a joke. But he heard Colton in his head. *Tell her what you're thinking, even if it sounds stupid.* He cleared his throat uncomfortably. "Why do you think she loved the rain so much, pixie? It meant spending time with her little sister."

Chapter Seventeen

Julie stared across the blanket at Reed, his words hanging in the air between them. A dozen thoughts swam in her mind at once. *I must not have been that terrible after all. If Serena suffered through rainstorms and boring card games just to be with me.* She'd had no idea until this moment that most of her insecurities stemmed from her distorted view of their times together. Her guilt had warped her point of view over the years. At that moment, instead of remembering her own whining and complaining during the card games, memories of them laughing hysterically, sharing confidences, pigging out on caramel corn, rolled through her consciousness as if projected on a movie screen. The rain pelting the glass in the quiet room made the memories come alive. She'd forgotten the good Serena brought out in her, only recognizing where she lacked. Where she differed from the perfection of her sister's memory.

Was it possible she'd been selling herself short? Was she

enough on her own? Just the mere possibility felt like lead weights toppling from her shoulders.

Julie came back to herself then, her surroundings returning in sharp focus. Reed, tuxedo-wearing Reed, watched her silently, a handful of cards tapping against his polished wingtip shoe, face partially obscured by shadows. Not shadowed enough for her to miss the intensity of his expression. He looked almost harsh in his attractiveness. The elegant attire suited him too well. She was suddenly thankful he didn't wear suits and ties to work like the other men. He'd be beating the women off with a stick.

Her gaze dropped to the blanket they sat on, one he'd put here specifically for her. To help her remember Serena. Such a simple gesture, and yet he would never know the impact it had. He'd started the ball rolling with his speech in the forest, and now for the first time in four years, breathing came easy. She didn't feel that insatiable need to find a task to occupy her mind, to relentlessly prove her worth. Could just sit there and *be*. With Reed. Yes, she wanted so badly to be with Reed. For as long as she could.

"Julie, I'm starting to get worried over here."

Laughter bubbled up in her throat as she launched herself across the blanket. Into his arms. He closed them around her tightly, releasing a shaky sigh against her neck.

"Thank you. For this."

"Oh, good." His body eased of tension. "You like it."

"Yes. Of course." She inhaled Reed's scent from his collar. "I love it."

When his fingers slid through her hair and pulled her back to meet his gaze, Julie leaned into his touch. Drawn to it. Craving it. Her mind, suddenly clear of gray fog, was on a high. At that moment, it became imperative that Reed share it with her. This man she cared about. This man who obviously cared about her to some degree, as well. Whatever their differences, whatever the future held, she needed him so badly her hands began to shake with the need to be touched. His hard body hummed with life beneath her, solid and warm. He felt her transformation. She could tell. The rise and fall of his chest gave him away, the way his mouth opened on her neck, hands tightening on her lower back.

"Reed," she murmured, finding his mouth, throwing every ounce of feeling within her body into the kiss. At the same time, her hands gripped his lapels and dragged the jacket from his broad shoulders. "I need you."

"You have me, baby." He watched her nimble fingers work his buttons with hot, anticipation-filled eyes. "You fucking have me."

"Here." She ripped open his shirt, revealing a rigid wall of muscle. "I need you right here."

"*Christ.* Anywhere." His hands slid up her thighs to disappear beneath her dress. Julie whimpered when he pressed his middle finger through the silk of her panties into her opening. She could feel the material grow damp as the heel of his hand ground over her clitoris. "You're going to take me right here. All of me. Where you're so tight and hot it makes me angry. Aren't you, baby?"

"*Yes.*" Julie's head fell back in surrender. With her current sharp focus, she could practically *feel* everything click into place with his demands. Reasons didn't matter. Only the sense of completion she felt when he took her over. "I'm going to take you. Where I'm t-tight."

Reed tore her panties, groaning a harsh sound. "Unzip

my pants. I want to see myself in your hand." She lowered his fly and his erection came free, thick and ready. Biting her lip to keep from moaning, she gripped him in her hand and stroked him root to tip. Reed threw back his head and growled at the ceiling. "That's my girl. Now guide me between your legs. I'm going to go fucking crazy watching you put me where you need me. You're clenching tighter just thinking about me filling you. Aren't you?"

Her thoughts blurred momentarily, then crystalized, centered on the pulse beating at the juncture of her thighs. His erection felt hard and heavy in her hand. With a moan of pleasure, she dragged him through the wetness at her core, circling the head around the bundle of nerves pleading for satisfaction. She took the condom he offered from his pocket and rolled it down his length quickly. The undeniable need to encourage him assailed her. To let him know the effect he had on her body in the way she knew he needed. Eyes locked with his, she sank her teeth into her lower lip. "I want to ride it hard, Reed. Tell me to ride it hard."

He took her chin between his thumb and index finger, tipping her face toward him. "Hard is the only way you ride it. *Ever*. Is that clear, Julie?"

She lowered herself onto him in answer, gasping at the delicious fullness. Her shaking thighs tightened around his waist until she got used to his size, then her hips began to rock. Hands clutching his shoulders for balance, she spread her thighs wide, bucking and swiveling mindlessly. Ceasing to think. His name became a litany on her lips, interrupted only when his fingers dug into the flesh of her ass so roughly she cried out. Her orgasm blasted through her in a rush, strengthening her even as it weakened her muscles and limbs.

Chest heaving, sweat beading his upper lip, Reed watched her in awe. A look that became an addiction on the spot. Julie pushed him down to the floor, smiling inwardly when he groaned at her boldness. She knew Reed liked to dominate. If she'd learned anything about herself this week, it was that she wanted, *needed*, him, exactly as he was. Right now, however, she needed something different. Something self-affirming. And he already knew her, cared about her enough, to give it to her. The thought caused an unnamed emotion to flood her chest.

"Keep riding," he encouraged with an upward thrust that made her gasp. "Finish me off, baby."

Emotions rocketing out of her control, Julie wanted to obey, but the girl she'd just rediscovered wanted to drive him out of control. Push him to his limit. Her hands rose of their own volition to unbutton the top of her dress, spreading the material wide so he could see her naked breasts. She ran her fingertips over the stiffened peaks, exulting in his harshened breathing.

"I can't hold back much longer. Take me or be *taken*, Julie."

She gathered the skirt of her dress in her hands and lifted. Immediately, Reed's head tilted forward to see the point where they were connected, jaw clenching at the sight. She raised up on her knees to circle her hips enticingly on the tip of his erection and watched his eyes go heavy-lidded. Then she sank down, slowly, inch by inch, until he filled her once more. Placing her hands lightly on his chest, she gave one leisurely roll of her hips. One designed to leave him wanting more.

He took it.

Reed flipped her onto her back and drove deep. "This what you want, Julie? It's what I want." He pushed her knees open and pumped his hips furiously. "Fuck that, I need it. Need *you*."

"You've had me." She dragged his head down for a long, wet kiss. "This whole time."

"My girl. *Mine*." He thrust one final time and came with a groan, face buried in her neck, muttering words that only made sense to their ears. They lay there for long minutes afterward catching their breath. Finally, Julie found the strength to lift her hand and run it down his back.

"Reed. A minute ago. Did you say something about the Super Bowl?"

His deep laughter shook her body, but he quickly grew serious. "Pixie, look at me," he commanded gruffly. She did as he asked, heart speeding up at the seriousness evident in his face. "You said in the forest, you don't know who you are with me. I hated it at the time. But the truth is, I don't know who I am with you, either. I only know I'm so much better. Stronger. Happier." He grasped her face in his hands. "You want to know what comes after this? Let me tell you what I should have said before. We go home together and find out who we are together. That's what comes after." His eyes held a hint of pleading. "Okay?"

Julie was already nodding. "I want that, too."

"Tell me this doesn't end. Tell me you'll stay with me and keep making me better."

"Yes. I don't want it to end." Julie kissed his lips softly, lingering there. "You had me the first night. You'll have me every night after."

"Move your things to my room. I'm not sleeping without you."

"Why can't you move your things to mine?"

"I feel another wager coming on," he murmured.

She nipped his ear. "You better not let me win."

Tenderness shone in his eyes. "Julie, you'll win all on your own."

Epilogue

Reed peered through the blinds in his living room for the hundredth time that night. With a curse, he grabbed the pull cord and yanked, uncovering the window completely. There. Now he could pace and watch for Julie to pull into his apartment complex at the same time. This had become his nightly routine and it had to stop. It *would* stop or he'd go insane. Every night, she finished work late, drove to her house to pack an overnight bag, and made her way to his place. Same routine. Every night. She never left anything behind, never asked for a drawer or a place to stow her hair dryer. Never left a trace of herself behind, except for her scent and the echo of her voice.

So he'd gone to her house tonight, gathered all her shit, and put it where it was meant to be.

Right beside his shit.

He had no idea how she would react. And yeah, maybe he should have talked to her about it first. But *she* was the talker in this relationship and she hadn't been holding up her end of the deal. Not where living together was concerned. They had returned from the wedding four months ago and hadn't managed to spend a single night apart since. God, he didn't even want to think about sleeping without her snuggled up against him, her blond hair wrapped around him like a safety blanket. She'd become his constant, the only source of pure happiness he'd ever known. She hid *nothing* from him without ever once demanding he do the same. Yet without even noticing it, he had. He'd wanted her to know about his past, to relive his close calls with her... wanted to be soothed by her.

That day when they'd played go fish in the rain, he'd told her he wanted to find out who they were together. He had his answer. They were permanent. Inescapable. They... shone.

Reed almost laughed out loud at the sentiment, so unlike him. This is what happiness did to a man. Made him comfortable with just about anything, all manner of unusual thoughts, as long as his woman came home, kissed him, and echoed the sentiment.

Goddammit. Where is she? Probably working too hard again, dead on her feet as usual. Reed started pacing again. As soon as she walked in and they got this living-together business cleared up, he'd put her into a bath with that fancy bubble business she liked. Coax her into eating something. Then he'd fuck her until her legs shook. Yeah. He needed her coming home to him straight after work, all right. It would eliminate an hour and a half at the end of each day where he had to be without her. An hour and a half per day that amounted to seven and a half hours a week. *Lunacy*, as far as he was concerned. The things they could spend those hours doing…the anticipation made his mouth go dry.

Lights speared across his living room, telling him she'd finally arrived. He went to the window to double-check and watched Julie exit her silver sedan. Their gazes collided through the window, hers questioning. His? Probably starved for the sight of her, mirroring how he felt at the end of every damn day. She would have gone to her apartment and found most of her things gone. If he hadn't left behind a deck of cards on her bed, set up for go fish, she probably would have assumed she'd been robbed. *Nope, baby. Just your crazy boyfriend who communicates best with playing cards.*

He crossed to his front door and opened it before she could do so with her own keys. "Pixie."

Eyebrow quirked, she opened her mouth to speak, but stopped. In a flash, she was plastered against him, head tipped back to receive his kiss. Their mouths moved hungrily against each other as Reed dragged her into the apartment and pushed her back up against the door. Those thighs opened up to receive him like a fucking dream and he grew so painfully rock-hard he had to release her mouth to drag in a ragged breath. They were always like this, hot and ready, but today he sensed something else behind her need, so he forced himself to refrain from kissing her. A nearly impossible feat.

Sweet. She's so sweet.

"If I didn't know better, I'd think you're trying to distract me," he rasped into her hair.

With a wicked glint in her eye, she worked her hips in slow a circle. "How am I doing, sugar?"

Reed groaned. "We're going to talk."

"There will be time for talk." She sucked at his neck. "I want to show you the new move I learned on Saturday at my pole dancing class."

"*Christ, Julie.*" Oh yeah, she knew all of his buttons and how to push them. Too bad he was stubborn as hell and today was the day she would agree to live with him, come hell or high water. He could face just about anything to get that outcome. Even resisting a lap dance from the sexiest woman on the planet. *His* woman. With a set jaw, he put a foot of distance between them. "Your things are here now. With mine."

"I gathered." He could hear her gulp. "You're supposed to catch burglars, not act like one."

Ignoring her barb, Reed tipped her chin up. "For months, I've been dropping hints, Pixie. *Months*. I bought new sheets, a bigger bed. I stocked the kitchen with all your salad nonsense. I had your name added to the lease."

Her blue eyes shot wide. "You did?"

"It's taped to the *refrigerator*." He gathered himself with a calming breath. "This is where you belong and you refuse to settle in. What do I have to do?" When her chin wobbled a little, Reed wanted to howl. Pain of any kind on her face felt like an arrow right to his heart. Unacceptable. He hadn't seen her upset in months. What had he done? "Julie, this is one of those times where you should be talking, but you aren't. Words, please."

"I knew you were dropping hints, but I didn't know if you meant them. I thought maybe you were just doing what you thought I wanted. What I needed." She squared her shoulders. "I'm the organizer. The planner. I don't want to jeopardize what we have by trying to push or fix or organize you. And I don't want to. You're perfect just the way you are. *We're* perfect."

His heart got stuck in his throat. "Julie—"

"I'm so happy with you," she blurted with her eyes closed. "It actually scares me when I remember you almost didn't come to the wedding."

Reed couldn't take it anymore; he needed to get closer. Now. He wrapped his arms around her and lifted her into a fierce hug. *Ah hell*, she was trembling. "I'd have found you one way or another. And I'm keeping you one way or another." He laid kisses along her hairline. "You're right. I don't need fixing. Neither do you. But we sure as hell *would* need fixing without each other."

She leaned into his mouth. "Things can stay the way they are."

"No. No, they can't. My wife isn't living in a separate house. I *mean* what I say."

Very slowly, Julie pulled back to look at him. "Wife?"

"Yes. Yes, *wife*. I asked your father yesterday." It took him a moment to find the words. How could he think when she was looking at him like that? Hopeful, surprised. Maybe even a little impressed. "I want to build a life with you, Julie Piper. You made me *need* this life, now you're going to live it with me. We're happy. We're going to *keep on* being happy. Do you understand? I've had you and now I can't go without."

He reached into his pants pocket and took out the ring. A pale-pink diamond. He'd seen it in the store and thought of the dress she'd been wearing that first night out on the patio. The night she'd sneaked into his room, knowing *full well* who was on the other side of that door. He hadn't even looked at any of the other ring choices. It had been made for him to give to her.

"Live with me. Marry me. All of it, please." He worked to steady his voice. "Your things are already here, anyway, and I'm keeping them."

She laughed through her tears, the sound so beautiful it colored the air around them. "Yes. I'll be your wife. Of course I will."

Relief moved through him so powerfully, he almost went to his knees. "Okay, then. Okay." He smiled. A huge one he couldn't contain. To cover his rare show of emotion, he threw her over his shoulder and strode toward the bedroom. "One more thing. You're not planning the wedding."

"Aw, come on, Reed…"

Grab the rest of the Wedding Dare series!

When four bridesmaids dare one another to find lust—or maybe even love—at the destination wedding event of the year, the groomsmen don't stand a chance. But little do the women know, the men are onto their game, and sparks will fly alongside the bouquet.

Four bridesmaids. Four groomsmen.
Five *New York Times* and USA TODAY bestselling authors. Long-carried torches, sizzling new attractions, and forbidden conquests will ensure a wedding never to be forgotten.

DARE TO RESIST
a *Wedding Dare* novella by Laura Kaye

Colton Brooks is in hell. Being trapped in a tiny motel room with Kady Dresco, the object of his darkest fantasies, will require every ounce of his restraint. She's his best friend's brilliant little sister, not to mention his competition for a lucrative military security services contract. Craving her submission is *not* allowed. But as her proximity and the memory of their steamy near-miss three years ago slowly destroys his resolve, Colton's not sure how much longer he can keep his hands off…or his heart closed.

FALLING FOR THE GROOMSMAN
a *Wedding Dare* novel by Diane Alberts

Photojournalist Christine Forsythe is ready to tackle her naughty to-do list, and who better to tap for the job than a hot groomsman? But when she crashes into her best friend's older brother, her plans change. Tyler Dresco took her virginity during the best night of her life, then bolted. The insatiable heat between them has only grown stronger, but Christine wants revenge. Soon, she's caught in her own trap of seduction. And before the wedding is over, Tyler's not the only one wanting more...

SEDUCING THE BRIDESMAID
a *Wedding Dare* novel by Katee Robert

Regan Wakefield is unafraid to go after what she wants, so she's thrilled when her friend's wedding offers her an opportunity to score Logan McCade, the practically perfect best man. Unfortunately, groomsman Brock McNeil keeps getting in her way, riling her up in the most delicious of ways. Regan may pretend the erotic electricity sparking between them is simply a distraction, but Brock will do whatever it takes to convince Regan that the best man for her is *him*.

BEST MAN WITH BENEFITS
a *Wedding Dare* novel by Samanthe Beck

Logan McCade's best man duties have just been expanded. Coaxing his best friend's little sister out of her shell should be easy—or so he thinks until he's blindsided by the delectably awkward Sophie Brooks. She's sweet, sexy, and brings much-needed calm to his hectic life. Soon, he's tempting her to explore *all* of her forbidden fantasies...and wondering exactly how far a favor to his best friend can go.

Acknowlegments

First and foremost, to my continuity mates: Katee Robert, Samanthe Beck, Diane Alberts and Laura Kaye, thank you. While I can't necessarily say this process was easy, it was FUN, thanks to your great attitudes and tireless work ethic. You were all an absolute pleasure to work with and I'm so glad I was involved.

To Heather Howland for helping this idea take shape (especially for pairing me with the broody hero), and Ellie Brennan who whipped my first draft into shape with flair, thank you.

To Beaver Creek Resort. You're welcome. We wouldn't turn down a free vacation.

To Google Docs and Excel spreadsheets and Yahoo Groups, thank you. This would not have been possible without your (occasionally unreliable) help.

To my husband and daughter, as always, for putting up with me when I'm off in fantasy land plotting when I should be enjoying your presence, thank you.

About the Author

NYT and USA TODAY bestselling author Tessa Bailey lives in Brooklyn, New York, with her husband and young daughter. When she isn't writing or reading romance, she enjoys a good argument and thirty-minute recipes.

www.tessabailey.com
Join Bailey's Babes!

Discover Tessa Bailey's NYT bestselling Line of Duty *series...*

PROTECTING WHAT'S HIS

Sassy bartender Ginger Peet just committed the perfect crime. Life-sized Dolly Parton statue in tow, Ginger and her sister flee Nashville. But their new neighbor, straight-laced Chicago homicide cop Derek Tyler, knows something's up—something *big*—and he won't rest until Ginger's safe...and in his bed for good.

PROTECTING WHAT'S THEIRS
HIS RISK TO TAKE
OFFICER OFF LIMITS
ASKING FOR TROUBLE
STAKING HIS CLAIM

Also by Tessa Bailey

UNFIXABLE

Willa Peet isn't interested in love. She's been there, done that, and has the shattered heart to prove it. Ready to shake the breakup, she heads to Dublin, Ireland. But there's a problem. A dark-haired, blue-eyed problem with a bad attitude that rivals her own. And he's not doling out friendly Irish welcomes. Shane Claymore is only in Dublin long enough to sell the Claymore Inn and get things in order for his mother and younger sister. Meeting a sarcastic American girl makes him question everything, but will their pasts destroy any hope of a future together?

Printed in Great Britain
by Amazon